VIOLA
IN REEL LIFE

ADRIANA
TRIGIANI

An Imprint of HarperCollinsPublishers

www.harperteen.com

Library of Congress Cataloging-in-Publication Data
Trigiani, Adriana.
    Viola in reel life : a novel / written by Adriana Trigiani. —
1st ed.
        p.   cm.
    Summary: When fourteen-year-old Viola is sent from her
beloved Brooklyn to boarding school in Indiana for ninth grade,
she overcomes her initial reservations as she makes friends with
her roommates, goes on a real date, and uses the unsettling ghost
she keeps seeing as the subject of a short film—her first.
    ISBN 978-0-06-145102-7
    [1.   Boarding   schools—Fiction.   2.   Schools—Fiction.
3. Video recordings—Production and direction—Fiction.
4. Dating (Customs)—Fiction. 5. Interpersonal relations—
Fiction. 6.   Self-reliance—Fiction. 7.   Ghosts—Fiction.
8. Indiana—Fiction.]   I. Title.
PZ7.T73512Vi   2009   2009014269
[Fic]—dc22   CIP
                                                               AC

Typography by Ray Shappell
09 10 11 12 13   LP/RRDB   10 9 8 7 6 5 4 3 2 1
❖
First Edition

For my dear reader

ONE

YOU WOULD NOT WANT TO BE ME.

No.

I'm marooned. Abandoned. Left to rot in boarding school in the dust bowl of Indiana like the potato we found in the cupboard in our kitchen in Brooklyn after months of searching for it. It was only when the entire kitchen began to smell like a root cellar from Pilgrim days that we figured out *why*—and when we finally found the potato it was soft, rotten, and breeding itself with white barnacles with totally disgusting green tips.

Consider me missing. Like the potato.

I only hope it doesn't take an entire year for people to miss me as much as I can already tell that I'm going to miss them. And if I'm not good at explaining it in words, well, there's always my movie camera. I do better with film anyhow. Images. Moving pictures.

I flip the latch off the lens, look into the view finder, and press Record.

"I'm in South Bend, Indiana, on September third, 2009."

With my hand securing the camera and my eye behind the lens, I turn.

Through my lens, I slowly drink in three old brick buildings: Curley Kerner Hall is the dormitory where I'll be living, Phyllis Hobson Jones Hall (called Hojo for short, according to my resident advisor) is the theater with art studios on the basement floor, and Geier-Kirshenbaum is the classroom building. The Chandler Gym, a modern building that looks like a Moonwalk carnival ride covered with a hard shell of white plastic, is obscured by tall trees on a flat field.

What did I expect? Purple mountain majesties? I'm in the pre-great plains of the Midwest. The gateway to the west. This *is* Indiana—translated it's a Native American word for *flat*. Okay, I made that up.

I film the freshly painted black sign with gold lettering set in a stone wall.

THE PREFECT ACADEMY FOR YOUNG WOMEN
SINCE 1890

It gives me little consolation to know that parents have been dumping their girls here for a solid education since bustle skirts, high-top shoes, and the invention of the cotton gin.

"This is my new school," I say aloud. "Or my own personal prison . . . your choice."

The stately brick buildings are connected by corridors of glass. From here, the glass hallways look like terrariums. That's right. The boarding school has glass atriums that look exactly like the scenes I made in summer camp out of old jelly jars filled with sand, cocktail umbrellas, and plastic bugs.

I pivot slowly to film the fields around the school. The land is the color of baked pizza crust without the tomato sauce. There are no lush rolling hills similar to the ones that appear on the school website. The babbling brook on the home page gushes crystal water, but when I went to film it, it was a bone-dry creek bed, with gross stones and tangled vines. Besides being marooned, I've been had—duped by my own parents, who, up until now, have made fairly intelligent decisions when it comes to me.

I lift the camera and film a slow pan. The endless blue

sky has gnarls of white clouds on the horizon. It looks a lot like the braided rag rug my mother keeps in front of the washing machine in the basement of our Brooklyn brownstone. Everything I see makes me long for home. I wonder what color the sky is now in New York. It's never *this* shade of blue. This is cheap eye shadow blue, whereas New York skies have a lot of indigo in them. When the moon rises over Indiana, I bet it will be a cheesy silver color, but at home, it's golden: 24K and so big, it throws ribbons of glitter over Cobble Hill. I can already tell there will be no glitter in Indiana.

The first thing my parents taught me when I held a camera was to spend the least amount of film time on beauty shots, and the most amount of time on people. "If you film people," my mom says, "you'll find your story." I slip the camera back into its case and head back to the dormitory. I'm going to remember to tell my mom that sometimes you need beauty—and beauty shots. Beauty makes me feel less alone.

The gothic entrance hall smells like lemon furniture polish and beeswax. The dorm has the feeling of an old church even though it's not one. Heavy dark wood stairs and banister lead to a ceiling covered in wide squares of carved mahogany. A burgundy carpet runner over the wide staircase is frayed at the edges but clean.

The hallway that leads to my room on the second floor is filled with small groups of girls, my fellow (!) incoming freshmen, who laugh and chat as though moving into a boarding school is the most natural thing in the world. I'll try not to resent the smiling, happy girls.

Inside the rooms are more girls, hanging posters and unpacking, talking as if they've known each other forever. But then there are the *other* girls, girls who are quiet and clump together, looking around with big eyes full of dread and fear waiting for something horrible to happen.

I guess I'm somewhere in the middle of these two camps.

I don't want to be too quick to make friends because I don't want to get stuck with an instant BFF who seems totally nice on the first day, and then a week later is revealed to be the most annoying person on the planet. I don't want to be *that* freshman—the chirpy kind, who needs friends fast in order not to feel alone. So I am deliberately aloof. At LaGuardia Arts, my old school, this method worked very well for me.

I did make close friends when I was a photographer for the yearbook. I even made my best friend since childhood join the yearbook staff. Andrew Bozelli (BFFAA—the double *A* is for: And Always) and I have

5

a lot in common. Never mind that everybody, I mean *everybody*, thinks we're boyfriend and girlfriend—we are *not* by the way, we just happen to spend a lot of time together. And we were both lucky enough to get variances to go to LaGuardia High School. I fish my phone out of my pocket as it beeps. It's Andrew.

AB: Unpacked?
Me: Yep.
AB: What have you filmed?
Me: Exteriors. I will download and send.
AB: You hate it already.
Me: Yeah.
AB: Hang in there.
Me: Trying.

Andrew and I sort of read each other's minds. We've known each other since Pre-K. His mom and my mom are friends, and they used to set a lot of playdates with the two of us because I'm an only child and my mother didn't want me to be antisocial. And she especially wanted me to play with boys so that when I turned fourteen I wouldn't find them weird, like they were from another planet or something. Mrs. Bozelli liked Andrew to play with me because she thought if he hung out with me, he would develop some "finesse."

See, Andrew is in trouble a lot at home because he's the middle son of three boys and gets blamed for everything. The bookends of the happy family squeeze out the middle like too much jelly between slices of Wonder bread. Andrew never complains, he says he doesn't mind. (I would, but what do I know? I don't have annoying brothers—or fun ones for that matter.) He just says, "That's the way it is," and he winds up spending a lot of time at my house, which is fine with me.

Although Andrew is my BFFAA, the true love of my life is Tag Nachmanoff, who happens to be the best-looking boy in Brooklyn. He's probably the most gorgeous boy in all five boroughs, but nobody I know *ever* goes to Staten Island, so let's just say in all of Brooklyn because I can be *sure* about *that*. The problem is I'm not the only girl who wants him—every *other* girl in school is crazy about him too.

Tag is tall and he has really wide shoulders. (He swims and flanks in field hockey.) He has black hair and really dark brown eyes and he's just so completely and totally handsome that it wouldn't surprise me if he *never* had a girlfriend because there wouldn't be anybody good-looking enough *ever* to match him. He should just wander the world alone—like some god from Greece or something, seeking truth and treasures—that's how gorgeous he actually *is*.

Tag maintains his distance. He practically invented the concept of cool. And he's older, and probably looking for somebody his age, eleventh grade (sixteen almost seventeen) instead of ninth (fourteen), which I am. I don't care about the huge age difference because Tag is *perfect* and I have proof on film.

When our school volunteered at God's Love We Deliver making dinners for the homeless and homebound, I made a movie of the whole day. Tag was the student coordinator, so I interviewed him for hours and then made sure I shot lots of him in action, ladling stew, making brownies, you get the gist. When I play back scenes of that day, it's hard to believe that such a boy actually exists in the realm of romantic possibility for any girl, much less me. He's hot *and* kind, and my mother says that's a rare combination in teenage boys and grown men.

Besides the mandatory schoolwide charity outing, I had a creative film and video class with Tag. One time, he was having trouble cutting some footage for an assignment, and I'm really good on the Avid, so I went over and helped him. He smelled like chlorine and sandalwood—very brisk and clean, like ocean water in a swimming pool clean. When I finished, he smiled at me and said, "Thanks, *Violet Riot*." Although my name is

Viola I never corrected him because I sort of like that he gave me a special name. And he says it *all* the time, *every* time he sees me—loud in the halls or when he passes in the lunch room.

Once, outside of Olive & Bette's in the Village where my mother took me to pick out "one thing" for my fourteenth birthday, he came by with his friends and shouted, "Violet Riot!" from across the street in front of Ralph Lauren. My mother said, "Who is that?" But I was really cool and didn't answer her. She said, "Well, he's a tall one." I just pretended that it didn't matter that we ran into TN. Truthfully, I couldn't believe that fate would have us both in the Village at the exact same moment in time. I mean, how can that even happen? But it did, and my friend Caitlin Pullapilly said that it was *a sign*. I miss Caitlin a lot. She's a very spiritual person.

The door to my new room, Quad 11 on the second floor of Curley Kerner, has a photo of my head floating on a construction paper cloud. Tacky. The resident advisor who decorated the doors is a senior named Trish, who is, like, eighteen and still wears Invisalign braces. This is a bad sign. It's the worst picture of me ever—she snapped it as my parents were leaving after drop-off—and I look like I'm dying. I didn't think she'd use it on my door or I would never have allowed her to take it. Now, I have to live with my head floating on a cloud looking like a bashed basketball with eyes so droopy from crying it looks like I have allergies. There are three other clouds, empty ones, to be filled with the heads of my roommates. I hope their pictures turn out as horrible as mine. I haven't had my head on a door since Chelsea Day School when I was, like, three years old, and it was pasted on a red construction paper balloon. Believe me, a cloud is not much of an upgrade.

I applied for the lottery to get a single room. Ten freshman girls get single rooms on the quad floors. I lost. So, I'm stuck with three roommates. I begged the school to put me in a single, but they honor their lottery so I'm out of luck.

Our room is pretty big, with three windows in a round alcove that overlooks the water fountain, which is three giant fish standing on their tail fins, mouths gaping, spitting water into a pool surrounded by a circular concrete bench.

We're on the east side of the building, which means this place will be loaded with sun. I actually like a cheery room. The furniture in our room is old but clean, two plain single beds with headboards, and a set of bunks. There are four small desks and desk chairs made of dark wood that look like they belong in a mental institution.

I went ahead and took one of the single beds, as I doubt I will be close enough to any of these girls to feel comfortable in a bunk-bed situation. My mom bought all my bed clothes in beige, thinking it would go well with whatever the other girls brought. For once, my mom was right. Not only won't I *clash*, I won't express any personal style whatsoever.

I place my camera on my desk and sit down on my bed, made perfectly in all its monochromatic beigeness by my mother, and text her.

Me: Thanks for making my bed.

Mom: Have you met your roommates?

Me: Not yet. Trish says that they will arrive soon.

On the edge of my seat in anticipation.

Mom: Funny.

Me: To you. You don't have to live here.

Mom: Give it 2 weeks. You will love it. I didn't like it the first day either but it grew on me.

Me: Whatever.

Mom: Dad and I are sorry we couldn't stay to meet the other parents.

11

Me: No worries. You had a plane to catch. I wish I was on it.

Mom: Will you text me when you start to like the place?

Me: There is no texting in Never.

I wound up in this particular boarding school because my mother went here, which is, like, the worst reason to go anywhere. That makes me a legacy even though my mom only came here for one year in 1983. She told me that in the eighties she had a separate backpack just for hair gel. I believe her.

"Excuse me."

I look up and see Marisol Carreras standing in the doorway with her parents. I know way too much about Marisol already because she writes a blog about her life and sent me the link when I received the letter with the room assignment. She's much tinier in life than she appeared online. She has a small body and a big head, like all the TV stars on *Gossip Girl* (which I'm totally not allowed to watch at home, so I watch it at Andrew's).

"I'm Marisol." She smiles big and wide, in a way that makes me feel slightly and instantly better.

"I know."

"Right, right. My blog." She blushes.

"I'm Viola Chesterton. From Brooklyn. New York."

Marisol is a brunette like me. She doesn't have high-lights or streaks or caramel chunks like the other girls that live on this hall. However, lookswise, I'm very average, whereas Marisol is a true exotic. Her hair glistens like strings of black licorice, unlike my brown frizzy hair. She has a noble profile with a straight nose, whereas mine has a bump and I may seriously consider plastic surgery down the line.

Marisol is also top of the class. She is from the South and she is here on scholarship. Her family are Mexican immigrants who live outside Richmond, Virginia, and Marisol is so smart, they had to send her *somewhere* because wherever she was wasn't *enough*. I can't believe the Prefect Academy qualifies as *enough* but whatever.

I get up from my bed to greet my new roommate and her family because I haven't left my good manners back in Brooklyn. I shake Marisol's hand and then her parents'. Her mother, also tiny, almost curtsies, while her dad, who looks a lot like the host of *Sábado Gigante* on the Spanish channel, shakes my hand and smiles. Marisol looks like both of her parents, but she inherited her big head from her dad. For those of us who faithfully read Marisol's blog, we know that her mom is a nurse and her dad owns a landscaping business called Ava Gardener's. My mom about died laughing when she saw that online.

"I took one of the single beds. I'm slightly claustrophobic," I lie.

"Me too." Marisol drops her duffel at the foot of the other twin bed. "So I'll take this one."

"Hiiiiiiya!" Trish bounds into the room with her pink digital camera and snaps a photo of Marisol for the cloud on the door. She looks at the picture. "Ooh, this is a good one," Trish says. "Hola, Marisol! I'm your resident advisor, Trish."

"Nice to meet you," Marisol says, blinking from the flash. "These are my parents, Mr. and Mrs. Carreras."

Trish fusses over Marisol's parents as she fussed over mine. Trish speaks the worst Spanish I have ever heard. It's all choppy and she uses her hands a lot. However, Mr. and Mrs. Carreras are very pleased that Trish is trying. I watch as she skillfully puts yet another set of parents at ease. They must learn that in resident advisor training. "I'll be right back," Trish says and skips out of the room.

"Wow." Marisol watches her go.

"I call her Trish Starbucks. She has more pep than a Venti latte."

"She seems nice."

"Oh yeah, she's buckets of nice."

Mr. and Mrs. Carreras look at each other, confused.

"Forgive me. I'm from New York. I'm a little wry," I explain.

Marisol speaks to her parents in Spanish, and they laugh really hard. Marisol turns to me. "My parents think you're funny."

"You know what I always say . . ."

"No. What?" Marisol asks as she unzips her duffel.

"If you can make parents laugh, you can probably get them to buy you a car when you're sixteen."

Marisol smiles. "I'll keep that in mind."

Mrs. Carreras opens a box and lifts out new pale blue sheets and a white cotton waffle blanket. Then she pulls out a quilt, which she places with care on the desk nearby.

I've never seen a person make a bed as quickly as Mrs. Carreras. I guess she mastered it in nursing. They have to make beds with people already *in* them, so they get good at it. When Mrs. C unfurls the quilt to go on top of the perfectly unwrinkled sheets and blanket, I try not to cringe.

"My mom made the quilt." Marisol forces a smile.

The quilt is babyish (the worst), with swatches of memorabilia sewn together. Things like pieces of

Marisol's first baby blanket, a triangle of red wool from her band uniform, messages written with permanent marker on pieces of satin—which Mrs. Carreras points out with way too much pride. It wouldn't help to turn it over because the underside is just bright orange fleece. The quilt says homemade like one of those crocheted toilet paper holders at my great-aunt Barb's in Schenectady. Our room is officially uncool—me with the blah beige and now Marisol with the homemade quilt of many colors. We're doomed.

"I'm back!" Trish says from the door, where she tapes Marisol's head to one of the clouds. It's as bad as the picture of me. Great, we're going to be the quad with the ugly girls and the ugly bedding. "Something the matter, Viola?"

"Can we redo the pictures? We really suck."

Trish squints up at the pictures. "You think so?"

"I look all sad and Marisol is just blurry."

Trish looks hurt.

"I mean, it's not the photography at all—you did a great job—we just need to comb our hair and put on some concealer or something. I look really red."

"You were crying," Trish reasons.

"Yeah." Great, she just told everybody that I'm on the ledge of insanity because I cried when my parents left.

Why don't I just curl up under Marisol's baby quilt and sob some more?

"I'll try not to cry when my parents leave," Marisol says supportively.

"You do whatever you need to do," I tell her, and I mean it. Marisol looks at me with relief, grateful for a little support.

Trish goes back to her room for the camera while Mr. and Mrs. Carreras say good-bye to me. Marisol takes their hands and leads them out into the hallway. I hope she'll be brave because I feel like an idiot that I wasn't.

TWO

OKAY, LIKE, SEVEN TRIES LATER, TRISH FINALLY GETS a decent picture of me for the door. It only took three tries with Marisol but she's photogenic, so even a total yutz with a camera, like Trish, couldn't mess it up.

Trish taped our new pictures on the clouds already so it's two down and two to go for Quad 11.

While I find Trish annoying, I do admire her ability to get things done quickly. You barely have your bags down around here and she's already got the door decorated. Maybe some of her follow-through will rub off on me, as I'm the Great Procrastinator. I don't know why, but I put off stuff like nobody's business. Hopefully that will all change here because there won't be the great city of New York to distract me. No Promenade, no Brooklyn

Bridge, no Greenwich Village, and no friends = no fun. Let's face it: South Bend, Indiana, will not be loaded with diversions. My mother, terminally upbeat and gratingly optimistic at all times, said something about enjoying the South Bend Symphony (please) and ice-skating on the Saint Joe River (the good old days) when she went to school here and perhaps I should check them out. Yeah. Right. I might just stay in my room and study so much I will rocket to the top of our class (doubt it).

Marisol set up her laptop on her desk with a brand-new desk lamp and she's writing on her blog. Evidently, she likes me a lot already, which is a good thing because the feeling is mutual.

The door to our quad pushes open, and with it comes a gust of chatter so loud it sounds like we're on the 42nd Street subway ramp at rush hour. Marisol and I look up from our computers.

"I'm Romy," the new girl announces. Romy Dixon, a peppy girl from upstate New York, has red hair cropped into a bob with two streaks of sky blue, which she tucks behind her ears when she's talking. The light blue streaks match her eyes. That's the only cool element to her look: From the neck down she is pure prepster—the straight-leg jeans lined in red flannel, a yellow Shetland wool sweater with her initials at the collar, and penny loafers (!) with no socks. It's like she walked out of Talbot's having spent the max on her holiday gift card on wool and plaid and shirts you have to iron with flat collars. It's September, and even though it's warm out, Romy wears the new fall line as though it's in a rule book somewhere.

Our newest and third roommate introduces us to her family. It will take an hour because Romy has, like, six parents. I'm not kidding. Her mother and father divorced and remarried, and evidently, her dad twice, so she has, like, three mothers. Only the current parents are here but it's strange, they all look alike. They wear L.L. Bean and have the ruddy faces of people who run for miles in cold weather. They also smell like muscle ointment, and they do not stop talking.

They carry all kinds of duffels loaded with what can only be sports equipment. From first glance, I see a tennis racket, golf clubs, and what look like field hockey sticks with socks on the shanks. Great. An athlete.

In the midst of their banter as they load the duffels into the closet, Marisol and I show Romy the bunks, and she snags the upper one. True athletes need air, apparently, and the top bunk gives her that breeze from the window transoms.

Romy's two mothers, with matching short haircuts,

make her bed, and they chat and laugh as though *they* are moving in. So much for divorced couples having issues and blended families unable to blend. These people seem happy. Marisol watches them, sort of amazed. She only has her original parents, as do I. Our families seem downright puny compared to this clan.

Romy's bunk is soon made up with a comforter that has a loud print of giant daisies in yellow and white on a field of black. The dads hang a poster of a tin crock of daisies over the upper bunk. (No matter where you sleep in this quad, you're gonna be looking at daisies. Great.) There is a throw pillow shaped like, guess what, a daisy (!) leaning against the headboard. Matchy matchy. Clearly, Romy planned this boarding school move for weeks. I pretended it wasn't happening until we got in the car yesterday and drove out here.

Romy is very take charge in a way that I find exhausting. Already. She has a round face, and what my mother would call "a determined chin." She sort of leads her parents around our room like it's a ring, like they are show ponies and she's the trainer. Romy tells them what goes where and how to hang it, fold it, or store it.

There's a knock at the door, even though it's propped open with a shoe box.

"Hi, I'm Suzanne." Suzanne Santry, the fourth girl in

our room, walks through the door. She looks around and flips her straight, champagne-blond hair back, securing it with a thin black satin headband. Her eyes are as dark as the satin. She looks like she belongs on a Los Angeles postcard even though she's actually from Chicago. I can't believe she's only fourteen, because she looks seventeen, easy.

Suzanne is totally beautiful, and for a moment, I imagine she might even be pretty enough for Tag Nachmanoff. She wears white shorts and a big baggy sweatshirt that says MARQUETTE. On her feet are very cool silver glitter flip-flops. My tan has faded already, while hers is still a tawny brown. She must moisturize.

"Do you mind the bottom bunk?" I ask her, now that I'm filled with guilt for choosing my bed and desk instead of waiting for my new roommates.

"Not at all." Suzanne smiles. "This is my mom, Kate," she says.

Suzanne's mom is tall and reedy, with an unfussy ponytail and clothes that say she has a day job in an office somewhere—a navy blazer, wool pants with a skinny black leather belt, and a silky shell under the blazer. Pearls are looped around her neck like she scooped them out of a treasure chest. Mrs. Santry introduces herself to Romy's parents (no small feat there), and then she makes her way to Marisol and me.

"Where's your dad?" Marisol asks. "Parking?"

"No, he's home. My brothers leave for Marquette tomorrow," Suzanne says, which also explains her sweatshirt.

"I'm solo." Kate grins, propping her reading glasses on her head like a tiara. "And I like it!"

Suzanne, of course, has the best bedding: a simple coverlet of navy and white ticking, with matching white sheets. She has a picture of her family in black-and-white in a silver frame, which she places on her desk. Suzanne has two older brothers (both hot and in college). They look like taller versions of two of the three Jonas Brothers (not Nick, the older ones). Suzanne's mom and dad have their arms around each other in the picture. Suzanne is stretched across on the lawn below them with her face propped in her hand. They look like they belong in the White House or something.

"I miss them already," Suzanne says wistfully as she straightens the picture of her family on her desk.

"Tell me about it," I agree. There's something about Suzanne that makes me want to agree with everything she says. She has that born leader thing, I think.

I dump all the footage I shot today into the computer and commence sorting shots to assemble. I plan on sending

Andrew, Caitlin, Mom, Dad, and my grandmother, Grand, regular video updates of my life in the waiting room of hell itself: Prefect Academy.

Trish finished decorating our doors by getting a good photo of Romy in three tries, and Suzanne in only one try. Trish thinks it's because she now officially has so much practice, but I say it's because Suzanne is incapable of taking a bad picture.

My roommates push through the newly decorated door.

"We loaded up the last of the parents," Romy announces. "And sent them home."

"Lovely." I focus on my screen.

"What are you doing?" Marisol asks breezily.

"Cutting some video I shot today."

"We just came from the welcome tents. They're setting up the picnic. It's going to be great!" Romy sounds like a cheerleader for dogs 'n' kraut. Let's face it. In her flannel lined jeans, she *is* a cheerleader for prepster picnic paraphernalia.

"They're having barbecue and homemade ice cream." Marisol sits down on my bed.

"Scrumptious," I say.

The girls look at one another and I see them laugh in the reflection of my chrome desk lamp. "What's so funny?" I turn around to face them.

"You. You're so droll," Suzanne says.

I can't believe they've already made a category for me. Droll. What does *that* mean? I just shrug. I mean, what can I say to *that*?

"Maybe you could film it. Our first dinner together and all." Marisol stands up and smoothes my beige chenille bedspread where she made a dent in it.

"We thought it would be fun if you made a record of our first night at PA." Romy looks at Suzanne and Marisol and nods as though they discussed assigning me to be the roving photographer at PA.

Oh great. When did the three of them become a *we*? And I'm the *them*—the *them* who stays in the room working on her Avid like some video geek who is finding something to do, a way to fill up her time, besides sitting around feeling abandoned, like that's some sort of crime or something. I get it. Suzanne, Romy, and Marisol have banded together to fight their feelings of loneliness. They've decided to be friends. The unwritten rules of boarding school are now being written without me.

"I don't know," I tell her.

"It would be so much fun to film the first picnic, and then years from now we can look back and see what we were all like." Marisol squints at my computer screen and critically analyzes the campus vista.

"I don't film for scrapbook purposes." How do I tell

25

these people that the last thing I want to do is waste my time filming boarding school high jinks? I'm serious about my camera. It's like asking Audrina Patridge to pose in her bikini for something other than publicity.

"Why do you do it then?" Suzanne asks without looking up from her BlackBerry.

"Make movies? I don't know. I always have."

"So it just comes naturally to you?" Romy asks.

"I sort of inherited my skill. My mom and dad make documentaries and the first thing I ever did was play with a camera. Or maybe it just seems like that. Anyhow, I've been making movies since I can remember."

"What do you do with the movies when you've made them?" Marisol asks.

"I catalog the footage." I call the film *footage*; this way they won't be asking me to take movies of them singing into their hairbrushes and clowning around in their pajamas in the dorm. Maybe they'll understand I have a deeper purpose. I'm not even going to tell them that I keep a video diary. Say the word *diary* to a teenager, and let's face it, you have a captive audience. But not mine—never—I've got the only eyes that will ever see The Viola Reels.

"I don't have any hobbies." Suzanne puts down her BlackBerry and lies on her bottom bunk, stretching her long legs until her feet rest on the foot of the bed. "I wish I did."

"I wouldn't call what I do a hobby. It's more than that. I'm preparing to be an artist. Someday, I want to be a filmmaker. A great one. Like Kurosawa."

"Wow," Romy chirps. "Who's that?"

"A Japanese director. But I probably won't ever be that good, so forget I said it."

"Knowing what you want to do with your life when you're fourteen years old is a sign of genius," Suzanne says.

I think Suzanne actually means what she says, or is it just because she's pretty that I believe every word that comes out of her mouth? "Thanks," I say quietly.

The freshman picnic is designed to help each new girl pretend that she has not left a real life behind, and that a party should automatically make up for all we've lost (as if). A bunch of picnic tables covered in tablecloths in the school colors, a fetching Kelly green and white, are arranged under a tent. There are big bunches of green and white balloons weighted down with rocks as centerpieces. My roommates and I get on the line for the food. We don't say much.

So far, here's the scorecard for sadness: Suzanne,

slightly sad; Romy, ecstatic and relieved to be in boarding school (probably because there are less people living in Curley Kerner than her real-life home, which is, like, packed with steps); Marisol, a little misty but happy to be in a place that will challenge her academically; and finally, me, miserable, annoyed, and generally feeling sick to my stomach. I take a plate off the stack and stand behind Marisol, who places some shredded lettuce on her plate. The buffet of picnic food—ears of boiled corn, big rolls, wieners on a spit, and vats of shredded beef/pork—reminds me how much I hate barbecue and how I'd rather be in Brooklyn ordering in cold sesame noodles from Sung Chu Mei and playing Rock Band 3 with Andrew.

The school is already trying to turn us into rah-rahs. There are cards on each table with lists of stuff to do that they consider fun. We motor through the meal and fan out to take advantage of the activities, which gives us something to do, instead of more time to think.

There are games to bring us together on teams (volleyball, badminton, horseshoes), snow cones to make (out of an old stainless-steel press that looks like you could cut leather with it), and ice cream to churn (we do the churning), and every once in a while, between the slurping and the cranking, an upperclassman comes through and stands at the podium with a microphone and tries to con us into joining clubs.

There's a swim team, a tennis team, a basketball team, and on the opposite end of the spectrum a Friday night pepperoni pizza club, which for me, sounds like the best group going.

Mrs. Patty Zidar, introduced as freshman advisor, is actually the school shrink. We had our fun (their idea of it) and now we're going to pay. She has, like, a billion numbered note cards with her speech on it, and we will have to listen until she reads off every single one of them.

Mrs. Zidar gets up from the picnic table, in her mom jeans and white button-down shirt tied at the waist, and smiles and adjusts the microphone. She's actually pretty with bright blond hair and clear green eyes. She goes in for the kill as we're now officially a captive audience full of sugar, exhausted from running around, and draped around the picnic tables eating our custom-made ice-cream sundaes.

"You girls are joining not only the amazing and fabulous class of 2012, but a legacy that includes Miriam Shropshire, Gloria Tucker, and Phyllis Applebaum . . ."

"Who *are* those people?" I whisper to Marisol.

"Who are those women you may ask?" Mrs. Zidar looks right at me as though she heard me. "They are women of substance. Miriam Shropshire is a concert viola player for the New York Philharmonic who founded her own classical group, Strings Three, which has toured internationally for three decades. Gloria Tucker was the coach of the 1972 Olympic javelin team, and Phyllis Applebaum was the first woman president of the National Association of Garden Clubs. . . ."

"This is the best she's got?" I drop my head on the table in total resignation. I guess Mrs. Zidar didn't get the memo: Women are leading corporations, and running for president and almost making it, and developing their own businesses, and being artists. It sounds so retro to bring up flower-arranging ladies. But all her talk about famous graduates is only to lead us into the real meat of her speech. She knows we have been dropped off, away from home for the first time, and while some of us might think it's great, some of us don't. She's trying to swing those of us who don't *do* the happy side of life to, well . . . the happy side of life. I would so be texting Andrew right now and telling him how boring and horrible this is if they hadn't told us we are not allowed to make calls or text during the picnic.

Mrs. Zidar drones on, using phrases like "separation anxiety," "in loco parentis," and "the golden rule" in a speech that now sounds more canned than the Boston baked beans I had with my black hot dog in the freezing-cold bun.

Our earnest RA, Trish, stands by the side of the tent, watching us. She smiles and waves when I catch her staring. It's been a long day, but Trish is still sparkly, like it's morning. I think Mrs. Zidar planted her there to show us that we've got someone older to talk to when we have nervous breakdowns or when the incoming freshmen finally realize that we're stuck here until next summer, which seems like a thousand years away.

The sun sets, taking the last bit of September heat with it. The Indiana sky over our picnic tent turns deep blue with streaks of lavender and orange. Some stray clouds move toward the flat line of the horizon. It's almost night and a chill goes up my spine.

As Mrs. Zidar wraps up her speech, and the sun disappears, homesickness spreads through the tents like the mumps. Night is always worst for sadness of any kind. The dark just buries you and makes you feel worse. Also, night seems to drag on twice as long as the day, and therefore gives you twice the amount of time to be upset.

Mrs. Zidar opens her arms wide. She smiles and says, "You will look back on these days with such affection. I know. I was in the Prefect Academy class of 1979."

"Did they have the same ice-cream maker?" I holler. Big laughter fills the tent.

"Uh-huh," Mrs. Zidar answers from the podium. "And I've got the triceps to prove it."

At last, Mrs. Zidar displays a sense of humor. As she gathers the cards from her speech, the freshman girls look around the tent, some check their phones (at last), some stand up, but most of us stay seated. It's as if no one wants the night to end, as if we wish Mrs. Zidar had another stack of cards to read through. We don't want to go back to our rooms and start our new lives; we want to go home, where we know who we are and what we like, where familiar might be boring, but boring is better than the unknown.

Romy, Suzanne, Marisol, and I head back to Curley Kerner in a clump. Now I sort of feel bad that I briefly hated them this afternoon. I've always had my own room. I don't like people peeping at my work, or having to worry if I put my shoes in the wrong place. They're not making me feel bad; I'm doing that on my own. My roommates are basically okay, and I'll take okay when I look around at some of the other freshmen who seem much worse than Marisol, Romy, and Suzanne. We don't have a giggler, a brainiac, or a snob in our group, so I guess I should count my blessings, which right now I can count on one finger.

When we pass the fountain, Marisol climbs up on the bench and runs around the circumference. Romy laughs as Suzanne follows. Suzanne pulls Romy up onto the bench after her. I snap off my lens cap and film my new roommates through the cascading water where little lights turn the water silver. It's a dreamy effect. I like it.

My desk has nails sticking up along the edge. I'll have to tell Trish so she can get me a hammer to pound them in. That'll give her something useful to do besides hovering over us like an older sister we didn't ask for. This desk is so old I don't know if it could even take the beating. It might end up as kindling for the next class bonfire.

I snap the cartridge out of my camera and load it into my computer. When my parents were my age, they had to shoot on film stock, and later would cut the film into sequences the old-fashioned way, on a Steenbeck. My mom thinks that the current way is superior to the old, though she says that the new technology has not made for *better* filmmakers, just *more* of us. Dad says that just because anybody can pick up a camera doesn't mean that they can play it like a Stradivarius. A filmmaker still needs a story worth telling from a particular point of view. We can shoot video for cheap, and swiftly edit on our computers, but that doesn't mean we have a story for an audience. I always remember that when I'm shooting a subject. *What am I trying to say?* is the question I ask myself a lot. That, and when I get to The End, *Is anybody going to watch?*

Marisol listens to her iPod as she lies in her bed flipping through a magazine. She wears new pajamas. I'm sure everybody will be wearing new pajamas tonight. I know I will. My mother got rid of my "Vote for Pedro" T-shirt and cupcake jam pants because they had holes in them. I'll be mad at her until the day I die for that one. This is one thing all mothers have in common. When it comes to boarding school, or sleepaway camp, or a visit with the grand-p's, a girl needs a new wardrobe from the underwear out.

Besides that, there won't be time to shop for clothes or anything else because we'll be too busy studying, and there aren't any mothers around to run to the mall on a whim and pick up something we might have left behind. You have to have everything you need from day one. My stuff is all packed in Ziploc bags and marked by season. My mother is very methodical that way.

Every once in a while, Marisol unconsciously sings a bar of music, which is irritating. If she keeps doing it, I'll have to say something. People who sing aloud while wearing earpieces should be banned from group living.

I slip on my headphones and listen to my voice-over, which I already recorded over the footage of my exile from Brooklyn. My mom films Andrew and me saying good-bye on the steps of our house in the neighborhood that I love.

The car is packed and Dad is motioning for me to get into the rental car the color of a ripe tomato. Mom hands me the camera as she climbs into the front seat.

I move the camera back to Andrew. He does this hilarious thing where he drapes himself on the wrought-iron fence in front of our house and pretends to sob like it's going to kill him that I'm leaving. He looks like Buster Keaton in those old silents that Dad makes me watch. I keep the camera on Andrew's histrionics as I climb into the car and shoot him out of the window until Dad makes the turn at the end of Austin Street, and Andrew ends up the size of a chocolate chip in the shot. Then, fade to black. Andrew Bozelli is gone. Or I'm the one who's gone.

I left Brooklyn two days ago with my parents. We drove through Pennsylvania, a bit of Ohio (staying the night in Sandusky), and then to Indiana, north to South Bend. It already seems like a hundred years ago. It's been just eight hours since they unpacked and left me, and I really miss them. It's only ever been the three of us, and I guess I thought it always would be. To be fair, my parents wanted to take me with them to Afghanistan. But they will be traveling with a news division filming a women's solidarity group and there was no way that I could be homeschooled, as they would be on the move. It's also dangerous—but I refuse to think about *that*.

Mom spent a "wonderful" year at the Prefect Academy when she was in the eleventh grade and is still friends with the girls she met here. Her mom, Grand, is an actress who was touring with the national company (bus 'n' truck they call it) of the Broadway musical *Mame* starring Angela Lansbury (who Grand adores). Grand was the understudy for the Vera Charles character, and there was just no way to take Mom on the road with her. Mom's father had remarried and Mom didn't want to live with his new family, so she wound up at the Prefect Academy.

The footage of my parents from this afternoon jumps onto the screen. I must have been nervous because the camera moves in fits and starts, like it has the jitters.

I first filmed my mom as she stood on the tree-lined avenue that leads to the fountain. Mom's hair was a mess from the car trip. She gave herself highlights from a home kit the night before we left, and they look like strands of red yarn on brown velvet on this video. My dad joins her, putting his arm around her waist.

My dad is losing his hair and has a strong profile, as sharp as a cartoon. He is handsome, my mom always says so. I don't think daughters can give proper assessment of their father's looks; he is just Dad to me.

My parents are a team—they met in film school. They are great cameramen, though Mom is a far better editor than Dad, who my mom says can be indulgent. I don't think that's true. My dad just likes the emotions he captures on film and doesn't quite know when to cut away and let the moment speak for itself. As I watch them onscreen, my eyes fill with tears. A year is a very long time to be without them. I wonder how I'll get through it.

I bet they won't even miss me after a while. I've been Princess Snark lately. (That's what Mom calls me when I'm just so over their badgering me about everything.) I can't help it. I have zero patience. Really. Zero. I can hardly stand myself sometimes, much less other people. I think it comes from trying to be perfect. Although I can't reach perfection, I drive myself crazy trying. Sometimes I wonder what will happen to me. If I keep worrying like this, I'll grind my teeth down into flat nubs like my violin teacher, Mrs. Doughty. She has teeth so tiny, you'd think she's part gerbil.

My mom says Mrs. D lost all her teeth from grinding (!) and now wears dentures, which scared me to death, like that could happen to *me* and *then* what? Mrs. Doughty's teeth issues were enough to motivate me to get a bite guard, but I don't think I'll wear it here. I don't want to be blah beige bedding/bad picture/bite guard girl. Can you imagine *that*?

I fast-forward to the footage of the buildings of the Prefect Academy. The gold letters on the sign came through clearly as I grabbed the late-afternoon light on the wood. Nice effect. I open the shot up wide and fill the screen with the slow pan of the fields. My hand is much steadier on this sequence.

Then I see a very weird thing. There's something on the screen that I didn't notice when I was filming the field outside.

In the distance, beyond the field, on the far property line of the school, I see something red move. A bird? I slow down the speed and look closely. It's not a bird. It's a woman. Strange. I don't remember a woman in the shot, and I don't remember anything red. She moves into the shot in full.

The woman wears a drop-waist red dress and a black velvet cloche hat. Her blond sausage curls bounce on the tops of her shoulders. She has matching red lips and tucks a small clutch purse under her arm. She wears black gloves with tiny bows on the wrists. She lights a cigarette and, turning away from the camera, puffs. She looks up into the sky, just as I did when filming the Indiana clouds.

"Whatcha doing?" Romy leans over my shoulder and looks at the screen.

I almost jump out of my skin.

"Sorry," she says. "I interrupted. You were concentrating."

"It's okay," I tell her, but I say it in a way that she knows it's not. "Romy, don't take this wrong, but I sort of need privacy when I'm editing."

Romy slinks away, her feelings hurt. I will make it up to her later. Right now, I can't worry about Romy because something crazy is going on here. I shot this footage this afternoon, and at that time there was no lady in the field. And here, on my screen, she walks in daylight. How did I miss her? What is going on?

I minimize the shot and save it. I'm too frazzled to figure this out right now.

Marisol looks up from her magazine. "Everything okay over there?" she says to me.

"Yeah," I lie.

I turn the computer off. I look around at my roommates. For a moment, I consider telling them about what I've seen but they'd think I was nuts. And there's one thing

I know after day one at the Prefect Academy—don't give anybody a reason to label you because whatever happens on the first day sticks. Just ask Harlowe Jenkins from Quad 3, who is now known as Throw-up Girl because she hurled in the bushes outside the picnic tent after she tried mango chutney for the first time on her hot dog. I bet she wishes she'd have stuck with ketchup.

THREE

WHEN I'M HOME IN BROOKLYN AND HAVING A CRISIS, I call Andrew and he either comes over to my house or I go over to his. But he's a million miles away, so I text him.

> **Me: Are you there? Mayday.**
> **AB: What's up?**
> **Me: I HATE IT HERE ALREADY!!!!!!!!!!!!!!!!!**
> **AB: LaGuardia sucks without you.**
> **Me: Thanks.**
> **AB: I got Roemer for math, Kleineck for English, and a new guy Portmondo for film (major suckage).**
> **Me: I get my class assignments tomorrow.**
> **AB: How are your roommates?**

Me: Natural beauty, prepster, and Latina.

AB: Intense.

Me: I know. I'd jump out the window but our room is on the second floor, which means I'd only break my neck and then be stuck here in traction for, like, a million years.

AB: So stay put.

Me: Not funny.

AB: Sorry.

Me: I'll never last here.

AB: Maybe it will go by fast.

Me: Maybe. Footage of you on the fence was high-larious.

AB: I stayed in character until you made it around the corner.

Me: Totally.

AB: Send it to me.

Me: I will. I also shot the school so you can check out the prison that is my life. It's not all bleak. I like Marisol a lot.

AB: Bright spot.

Me: I guess. Something really weird happened today.

AB: What?

Me: Got back and loaded the Avid and was cutting the footage of the school to show you, and a lady showed up

on film who wasn't there when I was filming.

AB: Weird.

Me: Very.

AB: Maybe you missed her?

Me: Maybe.

AB: Gotta go. It's my night to do the dishes.

Me: BFFAA.

AB: Yeah.

The shared bathroom on our floor is tiled white from floor to ceiling. Trish told us to always wear flip-flops on the tile because barefoot, it just gets too slick and we'll wipe out and break an arm or something. So far, this is the brand of good advice that the resident advisor shares with us. Priceless.

While I'm brushing my teeth, Trish pushes the bathroom door open and comes in, carrying her clipboard. "How's it going?" Trish leans against the sink and looks at me in the reflection of the mirror.

"Great." I spit my toothpaste into the sink.

"Tomorrow morning after breakfast, I'm going to take you guys over to Geier-Kirshenbaum Hall to pick up your class skeds."

I nod. Trish shaves the ends off of some words (sked for schedule) as though it takes too much of her overwhelming energy to finish them in a normal fashion.

"Coo?" Trish smiles broadly as she does it *again*, dropping the L off the end of "cool" as though it's done everyday. Her Invisalign braces give her teeth a hermetically sealed look, like cream cheese in plastic wrap.

"Cool." I force a smile on the L sound on the end of the word like I did when I used phonics flash cards when learning how to read. I don't think Trish picks up on it though.

"Viola, I know you'd requested a single room. I found out that one may open up, but it's not on our floor." Trish makes a big, fake frown. "Do you still want it if it becomes available?"

"Absolutely!" I tell her.

"But I wouldn't be your RA."

"I know. But I'm sure you'd get somebody nice in Quad 11 to replace me."

"Okay." Trish seems sad that I would choose to leave her floor. "I recommend you give it a few days before you move. We may grow on you."

Trish leaves the bathroom and I look into the mirror. You will never grow on me, Trish. Nor will this group living thing. Not ever. Never.

When I return to my room, Suzanne is already in bed (points for beauty sleep!). Romy is carefully folding her giant daisy comforter into a rectangle at the foot of her bunk. I guess she wants to keep it new-looking for as long as possible. Marisol is at her computer.

"Day one: Viola Chesterton held hostage," I tell them. They laugh.

I climb into my bed, which after a long day of saying good-bye, meeting new people, and that god-awful picnic is actually comfortable. I pull the blanket up over me.

"You may not hate this place so much in the morning," Romy chirps.

"Wanna bet?"

"Breakfast should be good. They have pancakes in the dining hall," Marisol says. "You can add stuff to them—raisins, chocolate chips, like, whatever you want."

I lie back and stare at the ceiling. "I'm stoked."

"You know, attitude is everything," Suzanne says from the bottom bunk.

Romy pipes up. "Viola, Suzanne is right. It's a hard adjustment for everybody. Your attitude will make the difference in whether you succeed or fail here."

"I'm sorry. Nothing against you guys. But I just love Brooklyn. I loved my school and my room and my friends. I didn't want a new school. I liked what I had." I turn over in my bed, hoping that this will signal an end to our discussion.

"You may end up liking this more," Romy reasons.

"Romy, I've only known you for one day, and already, you're way too upbeat for me."

She laughs. "So I'm told."

I drift off to sleep. At some point I wake up and check the clock. It's 1:15 in the morning, and I'm still here. I turn over and fold the pillow under my head. I close my eyes. I hear Suzanne blow her nose. I can't get back to sleep. For a moment, I think I might get up and turn on the computer and email Andrew. Sometimes I do that when I can't sleep. But I hear someone crying. It's Suzanne. She turns over in her bottom bunk and faces the wall. Evidently, I'm not the only miserable girl at the Prefect Academy.

The morning sun fills the alcove in our quad with bright white light. I push the covers off my face. For a moment, I've forgotten where I am. My bedroom in Brooklyn faces a brick wall and I never get much light, so waking up in boarding school is like waking up in a bus station. I feel totally public. I look around. I'm alone. The bunk beds are made. I look to the other single bed. Marisol's tacky quilt is smoothed over it. "Marisol?" I call out. No answer. I jump out of my bed and check the clock. It's only eight a.m. Where are they?

I go to my dresser and pull out a pair of cigarette jeans, a Bob Marley T-shirt, a sky-blue bandanna folded thick around my neck, and my jean jacket, because it's cold in here. I jump into my clothes, slip into my yellow patent leather flats, and grab my backpack.

The atriums are starting to fill with girls on their way to the dining hall. Some of them look a lot like me—the arty ones in jeans and hoodies—while the science/business/math brainiacs wear jeans with sherbet-colored sweaters with a white collared blouse peeking out. My shoes seem to be getting a lot of attention, and not exactly the kind I want. The girls look down at my feet like they're huge yellow taxi cabs instead of the coolest flats they had at Verve on 8th Avenue.

As I push through the crowd alone, I wish I'd have made firmer plans with my roommates for breakfast. Why didn't I hear them leaving? Why didn't they wake me up? Romy was so nice yesterday—she even forgave me on the spot for snapping at her when I was editing. I begin to make a list about how I'm going to change my ways at this school and start over with a better attitude. I walk quickly and sort of desperately alone, and promise myself that I will make friends with my roommates, so I never again feel this sense of sheer abandonment. It's a horrible feeling to be someplace new and on your own. I vow to film anything they ask me to, and to keep my bed made and my stuff neat, and my desk cleared. I need Romy, Suzanne, and Marisol. They're the only family I've got at this godforsaken school. And no family is perfect but I'll take them.

I push through the glass doors of the cafeteria. The buttery scent of pancakes, sweet maple syrup, and smoky bacon fills the air. I close my eyes and see my parents in our sunny kitchen making breakfast and my eyes fill with tears. I quickly wipe them away.

The cafeteria kitchen is open and is in the center of the room with the serving area shaped like an *L* around it. The bottom of the *L* is where you pick up your orange plastic tray, then follow the line as it snakes around cafeteria-style with windows filled with selections: individual cereal boxes dropped in small ceramic bowls, sliced fresh grapefruit, bananas cut in half, bagels. There's also an area to order hot food, like the pancakes Marisol was raving about last night. I make a note of where the line ends.

First I'm going to look for my roommates. I start at the tables closest to the door, round walnut laminate tables with orange, blue, and green plastic chairs around them. I scan them for familiar faces. Then I turn around.

Some girls look up at me. Maybe it's the bandanna, but they size me up real fast then go back to their breakfast. Finally, I see Marisol's shiny black hair pulled back in a braid. I wave. Marisol waves back, then turns to Suzanne who is dumping syrup on her pancakes. Romy sips her orange juice and looks the other way. I feel a freezing blizzard of a cold front as I weave my way toward my roommates.

"Hey, guys," I say as I pull out a chair. They greet me back, but it's not enthusiastic at all. "How are the pancakes?" I ask.

"They're good," Marisol says.

"You know, you guys could've woken me up. In fact, in the future, feel free."

"We didn't think you wanted to get up early," Suzanne says matter-of-factly.

"I went to the gym first and ran on the treadmill," Romy says. "I do that every morning."

I've never run for exercise in my life, but I'm not going to admit it. "That's great," I tell her.

"And I went on a walk around the campus this morning." Marisol smiles. "Trish gave a tour."

"Oh, I would have done that," I tell her.

"Really?" Marisol looks at Suzanne and Romy.

"Look, I know I was in a bad mood yesterday. . . ."

Just saying it makes me almost start to cry, but I stop myself. "I'm sorry about that. It wasn't anything about you guys—it's me."

Suzanne looks at Marisol, who looks at Romy. "Well, we thought . . ."

"What?" It sounds almost desperate coming out of my mouth.

"We heard you were taking a single room—moving out." Suzanne shrugs.

"It isn't definite."

"This morning Trish said the list cleared and that you still wanted a single." Marisol looks down at her breakfast. That Trish has a big mouth.

"Well . . ." And I don't know why this comes out of my mouth, but it does: "I don't have to take the room."

"You should if it will make you happy," Romy says.

"I don't know what will make me happy." My eyes sting with tears. I can't believe these girls have, like, talked about me and decided that I'm not worth fighting for after one day. *One* day!

"That was obvious yesterday. You seemed . . . annoyed." Marisol chooses her words carefully.

"We're *all* new here. You seem to forget that." Suzanne now sounds like a diplomat at the U.N. "It's hard for everybody. So you should do what's good for you because the truth is, we want to have fun in our room and we don't need an anchor dragging us down."

"I'm not an anchor. And . . . I wasn't annoyed at you." I turn to Romy. "Or you." I look at Marisol. "Or even you." I take a deep breath. "I don't adapt quickly to new situations."

Marisol smiles with relief. She looks at the girls. "I told you Viola had her own sense of humor. We misinterpreted her feelings."

"That's it. That's all. I was on the single room list when I applied. Now I'm here, and it's changed." I don't need to tell them even *I'm* shocked that I'm turning down a single. I'll look like a wing nut. I don't know how I'll feel tomorrow, but I know for sure that I don't want to wake up another morning and feel what I felt on this one. "I want to stay in our quad."

"Well, go get your breakfast. They stop serving in ten minutes. By the way, the pancakes are scrumpts."

I don't even mind that Marisol drops the end of the word just like Trish. I go to the line and pick up an orange tray. I load on my carton of milk and orange juice and napkin and utensils. I look over at the girls, who laugh and talk as though we didn't just have a totally intense conversation.

"What would you like with your pancakes?" asks an

51

upperclassman on work study wearing a chef's hat and a name tag that says "Shawna."

"Everything." I exhale. "Hash browns, bacon, hot raisins, syrup." I pile on a small paper hat of butter and another filled with peach marmalade. I don't even like marmalade, but I take it anyway. I'm going to fill my tray with food options till it's so loaded down and heavy it practically breaks my arms in half. Suddenly, I realize that I'm hungry, *really* hungry—the kind of hunger that can only come from being given a second chance.

"Wow. You don't look like a big eater," Shawna remarks.

"You have no idea," I tell her.

Caitlin Pullapilly's mother does not allow Caitlin to text or IM unless it's a life-or-death emergency. It's like 1990 for crying out loud, when it comes to communicating with Caitlin. What's next, Mrs. Pullapilly? Hello Kitty stationery and postage stamps? Please!

Caitlin and I have to send plain old emails—and only on a schedule—because at Caitlin's house, everybody shares one PC and it's in the living room so it's not like there's a lot of privacy. I think this is so lame. Practically all of Caitlin's relatives work in computer science. They are, like, geniuses and brilliant. Ridiculous that at home they live in the Old West when it comes to computers. So when I open my email there's a long letter from her because she has to get in everything all at once.

> *Dear Viola,*
>
> *I got your email about your new roommates. I agree you should stay in the quad. I don't think you should be alone in a room. You need people. Besides, they sound nice. Even though they are new to you, I'm sure you will grow to like them in time. Be a good listener. My mother always says this when I'm upset by other people's behavior and it helps me. Hope it helps you! LOL!*
>
> *Now, about your camera and filming the fields. Andrew downloaded the video you sent and it's so cool. I would probably never get to visit Indiana, and seeing it means I probably don't need to come out there. I saw the lady in the field in the red dress—who going forward, I would like to refer to as . . . the ghost, because I believe you when you say she wasn't there. In fact, when I zoomed in close up on her, she became so pixilated, she could've been a twisted red flag or blanket or something else like a parachute (sorry I'm not of much help).*
>
> *Right away I emailed my aunt Naira, who is a part-time mystic and a full-time veterinarian. You might remember her—she was at my last birthday party and*

she saved the life of our cat, Sir Mix-a-Lot, by perform-
ing brain surgery. Anyhow, without saying your name
I told her about the video you took and how a red lady
appeared in the far field. She agreed that the image
could well be a ghost! And she said that a lot of times
spirits live in old buildings (which for sure your dorm is)
and that you have to tell the spirits to move on or they'll
just stay. She also said to burn sage to get rid of the
spirits. That is effective. Aunt Naira said that spirits
stay in the earthly realm because they have something
to do. Let me see if I can find out more for you.

I have seen Tag in the hallway six times and at lunch
twice, which is pretty good as he's got AP classes and I
just have regular ninth grade. Tell me more about where
you are! Love, Caitlin

Dear Caitlin,

Okay. This is so weird. I don't think it's a piece of
fabric or a bird. I keep looking at it, and it seems more
like a woman. Ask Aunt Naira if this is just a fluke or
will the ghost be back, because if she comes back I'm
afraid I'll have a stroke. I can't burn sage—they don't
even allow scented candles in this school! Can I just
wave the sage without lighting it? And is it the same
sage that my mother puts on chicken? Like dried green

herbs? As for Tag, there are no boys here, so a couple
of times a day, I do look at the footage of him from the
God's Love charity day. Does he have a girlfriend? Find
out. Andrew refuses to ask anybody about Tag's love
life, which has slowed my reconnaissance efforts to a
standstill. Only YOU can get to the bottom of Tag's pri-
vate life, and I know you'll be stealth. Keep me in the
loop. Love, Viola, aka Violet Riot

I'm a little late to pick up my class schedule, but not so
late that anyone notices.

The lines inside the Geier-Kirshenbaum auditorium
are long. The longest are for admission into the gut
courses: Blog This; TV & Me, from *Lost in Space* to *Lost*;
and Makeup for Theater. These are probably all easy A's
but it doesn't matter. You can't sign up for them until
tenth grade. The freshman class assignments were made
prior to our arrival. All we have to do is officially register
and by lunch we'll know where we have to be.

"Whatcha got?" An upperclassman takes my computer printout of my classes from my hand. She's very
Upper West Side of Manhattan. Casual. "Wow. You got
Dr. Fandu for horticulture." She whispers, "We called it
ho-hum."

"Great."

"I'm Diane Davis." She extends her hand. "I hear you have a video camera and that you make movies."

"How did you know that?"

"Your profile."

"Oh yeah, right. I forgot about that." Now I could kick myself for being so eager to share my interests on the school Facebook page. What was I thinking? It's private of course, but not private enough if Diane could get her hands on it and then act all chatty with me about the information I put there.

"We could use your help for the Founder's Day events."

"Founder's Day? It sounds lame." I shrug.

Diane throws her head back and laughs. "It's not as bad as it sounds. We could use your expertise."

"Well, okay." I agree to help, but I feel like she sand-bagged me. The only thing I've signed up for officially is the pizza club.

"I'll email you," she says and walks away.

Marisol joins me with her schedule. She looks down at her list of classes with the books needed for each in bold letters beside them. "You wanna go to the bookstore?"

"Sure."

I follow Marisol out of the auditorium and down the stairs to the bookstore in the basement. We have most of the same classes, so we each pick up a plastic basket in the front of the store and, with our computer printouts as guides, begin to fill them with the books we need.

"I don't know how they can call this a store. It's a storage room with shelves in a basement," I complain.

Marisol gives me a copy of *The Poems of Gwendolyn Brooks* and an anthology by the poet Rita Dove. "And even paperbacks aren't cheap," I tell her. "They've got us right where they want us—we have to shop here. We can't drive to the mall."

"We can't drive period," Marisol reminds me.

"Besides the point. Don't you get it? We're retail hostages at this school."

"We'll survive," Marisol says. We load our math textbooks into the plastic baskets.

"Marisol, may I ask you a question?"

"Sure."

"Do you ever have a bad mood?"

Marisol laughs. "Yeah."

"It doesn't seem like it."

"Everybody has bad moods," she says practically.

"But what about you?"

Marisol looks up from her list. "I'm a survivor."

"You are? How, exactly?" For a moment, I imagine Marisol swinging from ropes on an obstacle course on a reality television show. I bet she could win; she has guts.

"Well, I'm Mexican and in Virginia, there aren't too many of us. So I had to learn how to make friends with people who might not normally know or like any Mexicans. It's sort of a challenge to me to make friends."

"No way."

"I'm always sure to speak first, and be friendly. And if I click with someone, I try to support them. You know, like I do with you and your camera work."

"That's very mature," I say thoughtfully.

"It's not hard to be your friend, Viola. You have a lot to offer. You're just scared. But we all are. So you shouldn't feel like you're the only one, because you're not."

"Thanks." If there was a basket by the check-out counter that I could fill with the shame I'm feeling right now, it wouldn't fit through the doors. I haven't taken ten seconds to look around and see what the other girls are going through. I'm a total Mimi. Me. Me. Me.

"Besides . . ." Marisol checks Walt Whitman's *Leaves of Grass* off her list, then looks at me. "Does it make it better to complain? I mean, we're here for the duration and I don't want to be miserable. Do you?"

I follow Marisol to the check-out line. And for the first time since I've landed at Prefect Academy, I feel a little twinge of belonging, as though maybe I can make this work until it's time to go home and go back to my real life in Brooklyn. It's just like my mom always says, "You can make friends anywhere in the world. Just say hello." Well, this is taking a lot more than just hello, but I'm starting to get the hang of it.

FOUR

Dear Mom and Dad,

Well, you were sort of like maybe half right about me adjusting to PA. It's almost a month or a quarter way into the term and I'm starting to almost sort of actually like it here. I played pick-up basketball with the girls from my hall after dinner tonight. I just sort of grabbed the ball and started dribbling. My days on the public court by LaGuardia really paid off as I'm one of the only girls here who can do a proper layup (omitting the varsity team of course). Anyhoo, (that's Indiana for a Brooklyn vamp) I'm doing okay in my classes. So far. The teachers are on the lookout for any girl having what looks like a mental breakdown due to homesickness or anything else that's tragic. I'm pretty lucky. I haven't had a crying jag in the library yet. But maybe it's coming. Who knows? I sure wish I was with you. And please, Mom, don't let Dad hog the footage you've shot. Send it and let me see what you're seeing. Dad is, like, way too much of a perfectionist and he'll wait till the job is completely done before he shows me ANY footage at all. Afghanistan is in the news, like, every day over here. I have it on auto-news pop-up. I liked the pix of your layover in London. I could use some of those scones and clotted cream you had at that tea room called Nigel Stoneman's. It looked delish. As for the food: The breakfast here is the best, so I load up then. Scrambled eggs, hash browns, and a doughnut machine. Lunch is salad bar and stuff, and dinner is like casseroles that Grand makes when four billion people are coming over to her apartment after the theater. You know, ground beef, cheese, and mystery sauce. Oh, and I might do something with Founder's Day stuff. More to come on that later. That's all I got for now. Love you both, V.

Mrs. Carleton is one of those teachers who, when you're sitting in class and only half listening, you imagine a beauty makeover for her. She has potential with nice features like pretty brown eyes and brown hair and a petite figure. But her eyes are all bleary and red from being up all night (she has a new baby), and her haircut is a bob that's all uneven on the bottom (she probably cuts it herself with nail scissors), and she wears khaki pants with a baggy seat and one of those XL sherbet-colored sweaters that seem to be so popular on the Indiana side of the dividing line of the French and Indian War. She starts out the period wearing peach lip gloss, but by the end she's bitten it all off, and then she has absolutely zero makeup on.

Mrs. Carleton requires us to leave all cell phones and BlackBerrys in a basket on her desk before class begins. On the first day of class, a couple girls left their phones on vibrate and the vibration actually made the basket walk off the edge of her desk and fall on the floor with the phones going everywhere. All twelve of us ran to pick up our phones to make sure they weren't damaged. Now, when Mrs. Carleton collects the devices, she leaves the basket on the floor by the door so if anything vibrates it will just shake the basket, not hurl it into infinity and beyond.

Mrs. Carleton wakes me from my daydreams of makeovers. "Viola, tell us about the ghost in *Hamlet*."

"Well, he's Hamlet's father, who was murdered by his brother. Now the evil brother will be king in Hamlet's father's place."

"Why do you think Shakespeare chose a ghost to deliver the prologue?"

"Well, he probably needed a character to get everybody in the audience up to speed. And a ghost is as good a way as any."

Marisol raises her hand. "It was inventive."

"And why is that?" Mrs. Carleton leans against the desk. Her khakis are baggy in the front too, where her knees bend. I don't even know how you'd fix *that* saggage problem in a beauty/fashion makeover. You'd probably just have to spring for new pants.

"When someone dies in real life, sometimes the essence of that person remains," Marisol says.

"That's very interesting, Marisol, the idea that a person's essence lingers in the ether after they have died."

"It's creepy," I blurt. The girls in the class laugh.

"It's supposed to be creepy." Mrs. Carleton paces before the class. "The father has been murdered but he wants to help his son, who is still living, make important decisions, so he appears to warn and to guide him."

Mrs. Carleton checks the clock. "I think this is an excellent avenue for our next discussion. I'd like you girls to research the role of the supernatural in *Hamlet* and write a one-page essay about it for our next class. Here's a hint, I happen to know there is an e-book of an old book called *Life in Shakespeare's England* in the library. And I'd like you to take a stand in your essay. Argue that there are ghosts, or argue that there can't be. And back it up with research."

At the end of class Marisol and I stand on line waiting to pick up our phones. We pick them up and commence scrolling through our messages as we walk out of the building and into the cold. There's a text from my grandmother.

> **Grand: Your mom and dad tell me you're adjusting.**
> **I sent cookies. I didn't bake them. Balducci's did.**
> **Love you.**

"Newsflash. Cookies coming from my grandmother," I tell Marisol.

"Great." Marisol tucks her phone into her pocket.

"She didn't bake them but they're not exactly store bought. She got them at Balducci's and they make their own food. So it's sort of homemade, once removed."

"I'm sure they'll be delicious," Marisol says.

This is definitely something to like about Marisol. It takes very little to please her. There is not an ounce of snark in her entire body, and just the word *cookies* puts a smile on her face. I wish I had some of that bottomless cheer.

I text Grand.

Me: Rockin' on the cookies. Do you know anything about the ghost in *Hamlet*?
Grand: Played Ophelia at the Cincinnati Playhouse in the Park. Glorious production directed by Ed Stern.
Me: Cool. May need to pick your brain later.
Grand: Anytime! xoxox

"How many people have an actual actress for a grandmother?" Marisol asks. "That's so cool."

"She's a character. That's what my dad always says about her. And I always found that such a funny thing to say: Grand is a character and she plays them. How weird is that?"

"It's fabulous. Are you kidding?" Marisol smiles.

"She's been on Broadway. But you know? She doesn't even care *where* she acts, just so she gets to be in a play. She even loves dinky productions where she travels to Queens and they lift up the back of a truck and turn it into a stage and she does monologues from the classics for free. She is totally game for anything."

We walk to the dining hall as fall leaves, gold and red, swirl around us in the wind. They crunch under our feet on the winding sidewalk. Sometimes the Prefect Academy is downright pretty. Like now. It's twilight and all of our campus turns deep blue. The lights from the dorm flicker in the distance like stars. The air is crisp and smells like sweet vanilla.

I'm lucky that I have most of my classes with Marisol. I think they deliberately put a Brooklyn girl with a Mexican girl for a reason. Diversity. Marisol and I have discussed it.

Marisol misses Richmond a lot, and her grandmother who lives in Mexico. It's hard for her as the days get colder. She's a warm-weather person, which is why it's so insane that out of all the boarding schools in the world, she picks this one in freezing South Bend, Indiana. I don't mind winter and I sure don't mind autumn at all, because it means soon it will be Christmas break, and I can see my parents and my friends and eat sesame noodles until my stomach explodes.

We bury our hands in our pockets and make our way down the path. "Do you believe in ghosts?" I ask Marisol.

"I don't know. Do you?"

"For sure. My friend Caitlin Pullapilly says there's a whole pecking order in the spiritual world. They have pictures and everything. She's Hindu."

"Cool." Marisol shrugs.

I haven't thought about ghosts much since that first night when I was looking at the footage and saw the Red

Lady. It's a funny thing—when something like that happens, and you can't explain it, you put it aside in your thoughts and then, as the days go by the memory of it fades and I wonder if it *ever* happened. Maybe I *did* make it all up.

I was so freaked out that first day—it was probably my imagination playing tricks on me. At any rate, I've decided I'm not a very spiritual person. I don't really know about other worlds, times, and places—though I sort of wish that all that stuff were true. If it were, it would mean that time as I know it doesn't exist, that my mother and father aren't half a world away, that Tag Nachmanoff really isn't too old for me, and that the hands on the clock are spinning so fast that I'm already back home at LaGuardia and in my old routine.

"Can I tell you something?" Marisol pulls her hat down over her ears.

"Sure."

"I hate Shakespeare."

"Me too," I admit. "Why do they teach it?"

"It's classic literature."

"Who said so?"

"Everybody. I mean, every school teaches Shakespeare."

"Maybe it's just us." I shrug.

67

Marisol pushes open the door to the dining hall. We are greeted by peals of laughter and loud conversations as pretty much every girl from ninth through twelfth grade is either on the line to pick up their dinner or at the salad bar or already at their tables eating.

A warm blast from the overhead heater by the entrance warms us as we go in. It's tetrazzini night and I can see wedges of apple pie for dessert. Yum.

Marisol and I usually study the forthcoming menus in the online school newsletter as though we are archaeologists on a dig unearthing something wonderful—we discuss it, ruminate, and get excited when the menu lists something we like.

Marisol hands me an orange tray, and places her own on the ledge, filling it with utensils and a napkin.

I wave at Suzanne and Romy, who have saved seats for us by the window at what has become *our* table. It's so funny. My mother told me it would take exactly two weeks for me to like the place. It's been almost a month (let's face it—I'm a hard sell) and I guess boarding school is sort of growing on me. It's little things, like dinner with my roommates when it's cold outside, or assembly on Fridays when they have lame speakers and we drive them nuts with questions afterward, or in class, when I'm learning something I know I'll use in life—these are the moments when I know I kind of like it here.

Prefect Academy has turned into a family in a strange way with many moving parts and different points of view. Yet, we crave the familiar and stake out our tables and seats and sit in the same ones every night. All the girls do. It's part of a routine now, and it reminds us that we depend upon one another now, and whatever makes us feel secure is best.

Marisol and I wave to our neighbors from down the hall.

"Did you hear about Missie Cannon on Third South?" Marisol whispers. "She went home to Pennsylvania."

"What happened?"

"She was caught drinking."

"You're kidding."

"Nope. She's in tenth grade and she snuck in a bunch of wine coolers and gave them out and somebody reported her."

Marisol and I lift our trays and snake through the round tables to our roommates.

"Okay, we're all going to this." Romy holds up a flyer.

DANCE
Freshman girls are invited to attend!
November 15, 2009

Grabeel Sharpe Academy for Boys
Lakewood
Buses depart at 6 p.m.

"I am *not* going to Drab Dull for a dance," I tell the girls as I put down my tray and backpack.

"What's Drab Dull?" Romy asks.

"It's like the law of the jungle at PA," I explain. "I hear the upperclassmen say it all the time. Finally I asked one of them what it was, and she explained that's what generations of girls have called our brother school. So count me out. I'm not going."

"Oh, probably some disgruntled girl got burned by a Grabeel Sharpe guy a hundred years ago, and she started a campaign to diss the school forever. Guys can be idiots. But not *all* guys," Suzanne says diplomatically.

I'm not about to explain the real reasons I won't get on that bus and go to their dance. They do not need to know that I will never go to a dance until I can go with the likes of Tag Nachmanoff. I don't settle in any other area of my life when it comes to excellence, so why should I lower my standards when it comes to boys? I don't use a crap camera, I don't eat junk, and I'm not going to a dance where the boys are bores.

"You snap judge," Marisol says to me.

"I do not," I say, taken aback.

"Viola, you *totally* snap judge. You thought Mrs. Carleton was a fashion disaster because she wears Land's End khakis."

"I modified my position when she wore Levi's."

"I know. But you still had a week where you were doubting everything she said in class because she didn't dress cool."

"You make me sound awful."

"If the yellow patent leather flats fit . . . ," Suzanne jokes.

"I haven't worn them since the first day," I say defensively.

"Everybody makes mistakes," Romy says. "Even you."

"Okay, okay. I suck. I get it."

"Not in every way. Just in your snap judging," Marisol says kindly.

"Viola is slightly sheltered," Suzanne says in a matter-of-fact tone.

"What does that mean?" I'm almost shouting, my anxiety level on orange.

"Oh, don't worry about it. It just means that you're an only child, and you don't have siblings who push you to do things."

"Okay. Fair enough." I shrug.

"Look, here's the deal about boys," Suzanne begins.

Marisol, Romy, and I lean in, because in our universe, Suzanne is The Great and Tall Blond One, who knows much more than we do about the intricacies of romantic relationships. She's definitely got the upper hand when it comes to boys and there are two reasons for that. One, she has two older brothers who are hot and in college, and two, pretty girls like Suzanne are pursued, so they get to pick the boys they want first. It's not like they ever pine, because they don't have time to. They're too busy fielding offers. I guarantee you that Suzanne does not have a Tag Nachmanoff–style crush on any boy in Chicago. She is way too cool to waste her time on something that might never happen. So when it comes to boys, dances, and the players at Drab Dull Academy, we have to defer to Suzanne. She has an inside track.

"It's not like you have to go out with these guys or even see them every day. This is a *dance*. It's a chance to shake things up and make new friends who happen to be boys. They are not a separate species. When it comes to boys, we all need practice. We're at an all-girl boarding school, and our options are limited. So, let us all be open to the possibilities. We'll talk. We'll dance. Maybe one of us will even kiss a cute one."

I lean back in my chair. I think we can all guess who would come away from this dance having been kissed. It won't be Romy, it won't be Marisol, and it surely won't be me. But Suzanne will do everything she can to convince us that we should *try*.

The dance that I wasn't ever going to attend in about a jillion years just turned into a make-out session with random boys we have never met. The pressure is almost too much to bear except that I really do want to kiss a boy that I like—and when the time comes, I don't want to be bad at it. It makes sense that there should be some practice involved, or at least the development of the skills that lead up to kissing. Now, this could be a plus to being in Indiana. I could practice here and then when I go home to Brooklyn I'll be a pro. But any way around it, I am already in the presence of a girl with wisdom and experience. Suzanne knows what she's talking about.

"Now . . . ," Suzanne continues, "you absolutely are not required to kiss any boy just to kiss them. It's not like there's a scorecard or anything."

"Really? We're being herded onto a bus to drive across town to an all-boy academy where we disembark and join our lonely counterparts on a dance floor. Sounds like a scorecard situation to me." I salt the tetrazzini.

"You're making way too big a deal out of this," Suzanne says. "We should be talking about what we're going to wear, not about how we're going to feel. Who cares about that? If it sucks, and the boys are idiots, we always have each other."

"I'm in," Romy says solemnly.

"Me too." Marisol jabs me with her elbow.

"Okay, okay. I'll go." I stab my apple pie to take a bite because I oversalted the tetrazzini. I wonder what my mother would say about eating dessert for dinner, but that's the beauty of boarding school. I make all my own decisions, small and medium, while the big ones are left up to the Prefect Academy—and as far as boys go, to the only expert I know: Suzanne Santry.

"Hi, honey! We're in Wardak. It's near Kabul." My mom waves into the video conference camera on my computer. "You look great!" Mom moves in toward the eye of the camera, her face so close to the screen, she fills it. It's such a tight shot, our dentist, Dr. Berger, could examine her molars.

"Viola, how are you?" My dad moves into the frame, pushing my mom aside.

I look around my dorm room to make sure none of my roommates are lurking. "There's a school dance coming up," I tell them.

"How fabulous!"

One of my mom's worst traits is that she gets excited about things like school dances.

"Ugh."

"Now, Vi, attitude is everything when it comes to your social life." Mom bites her lip and sinks back in the frame, while Dad leans forward to deal with me. His forehead wrinkles up in small lines like a tree trunk.

"Your first dance." Dad smiles.

"And it may be my last! Princess Snark lives!" I make a tiara on the back of my head by waving my fingers.

"So does your sense of humor. I think you like the idea of this dance," Dad says teasingly.

I just shrug.

"I'm going to let you two talk for a moment." Mom looks at Dad and then goes out of frame.

"Oh, Dad."

"Your mother thinks we should have a talk."

"About what?"

"Boys," Dad says.

"I know all about them," I promise. "I mean, Andrew is a boy—and you used to be one—how much do I need to know?"

"Good point. We're just people."

"Yeah."

"Just talk to everybody and have a good time," Dad offers.

"Great advice, Dad. If I had a personality like that, I could follow your instructions."

Dad laughs. Mom comes back into the frame. "I didn't listen to a word of that," she lies. "So, how are your roommates? How's Soledad?"

"Marisol," I correct her.

"Right, right. I loved her blog."

"I like Marisol a lot. We have a lot of classes together. Suzanne is, like, totally pretty and nice. Romy talks nonstop."

"Maybe she's nervous," Mom says.

"No, she just likes to talk," I say.

"It's good to be around upbeat people."

"I guess."

"Have you been working on your video diary?"

"Oh yeah. The Viola Reels. It's going great. I'm kind of known for my camera now. That's how I've been dragged into working on Founder's Day."

"Oh, you'll love it. The girls dress up in costumes that are the uniforms from every era in the school's history," Mom says.

"I know all about it. I'm helping with the play. I'm

doing computerized scenery."

"How wonderful!" Mom actually claps her hands.

"How are the classes?" Dad asks.

"The teachers are totally Midwestern."

"You're in the Midwest, Viola," he reminds me.

"That's the problem. South Bend, Indiana, will never be Brooklyn, New York. Indiana has its charms. I like twilight. The girls are growing on me. The hash browns are most excellent. But I miss home. I miss stuff. Like, I miss our house. I miss our stoop where people leave cards for emergency locksmith service and stacks of flyers for Indian food to go and discount coupons for Tel Aviv airport rides. I miss Andrew. I miss Caitlin, even though her mother is way too strict and annoying. I miss LaGuardia. I miss Ray's Pizza and the Manhattan skyline at night from the overlook at Dumbo. I miss gummi worms in Ziplocs from our bodega. I miss the garden on Clark Street where they planted sunflowers that got as tall as the second-story windows. I miss taxi cabs and gyros and frozen hot chocolate from Serendipity on Saturdays. I miss the fountain at Lincoln Center in December and the ballerinas in their leg warmers on their way to a Nutcracker matinee. I miss Mr. Sandovitch in his tuxedo when the car service comes to pick him up with his ginormous bass fiddle to play a classical concert at the Steinway Hall. I miss New York. I miss Brooklyn. I miss the subway. I miss you."

"We miss you too, honey," Dad says.

"With all our hearts," Mom adds.

"Then fly me over there. I can be very quiet in Afghanistan. I can do some amazing handheld camera work. You know I can do it!"

"Viola, someday you'll be able to travel with us." Dad looks at Mom and then back into the eye of the computer camera. "And even make movies with us. But right now, it's best for you to have an experience like boarding school. I promise that it will open you up in ways you never imagined."

"It was so good for me, Viola. I know it will be good for you." Mom nods slowly.

"Okay, okay." The notion of what might be good for me makes tears come to my eyes. I wipe them on my sleeve. Dad and Mom reach out and touch the camera on their end, and I do the same on mine. For just a moment I can feel their hands on mine, and a rush of warmth and security and love washes over me like autumn rain. As the screen goes to black, I remember that a year is just a year, even though it seems like so much more, like a forever and always more.

* * *

I took a risk before I came to PA and had my bangs cut—and the results were more Pippi Longstocking (bad) than Hayden Panettiere (perfect) so I'm using this time wisely by growing them out, and practicing my dance skills in gym—just in case I will actually *dance* at a thing called a dance.

I think my bangs will have time to grow before the dance if I don't get tempted to cut them short when they start to get in my eyes. That is the problem with bangs—there's a lot of upkeep involved. Growing hair out is a lesson in patience. Scientists have confirmed that human hair grows on an average of half an inch a month, so I'm about six weeks away from the tops of my ears.

"Are you ready to go?" Trish pokes her head in the doorway.

"Yep." I stuff my laptop into my backpack.

"It's really nice of you to help with Founder's Day."

"No problem. I think it's important to understand what you come from in order to move forward. That includes the history of the Prefect Academy."

Trish thinks for a moment and then smiles. "You're joking, right?"

"Trish, you're onto me," I tell her.

We head over to Hojo. Trish is growing on me. She helped Romy through a bout of food poisoning, took

Marisol over to the infirmary when she was starting to get a case of carpal tunnel syndrome from all her key padding, and best of all, she remembered Suzanne's birthday and baked a cake for her. And it was good. Trish is on her game as an RA and when I see how some of the other resident advisors act around here, I'm glad we ended up with her. She is someone you can interrupt any time, day or night. And *that* is a gift.

"Aren't you glad you didn't take that single?" Trish says as we walk.

"Uh, yeah."

"You hesitated."

"It was a comic beat, Trish."

Trish thinks a moment and then laughs. "You're a pip, Viola. Room forty-seven." Trish motions for me to follow her.

There's a portrait of Phyllis Hobson Jones over the entrance that is post-modern. It's done with a bunch of tiny stones, pointillist almost, in an enormous frame.

Phyllis had a real 1950s face: simple red lips, pageboy hairstyle, and wide-set eyes full of wonder. Would she think it was funny that we call the hall named after her Hojo, or would she be insulted? Women as beautiful as Phyllis rarely have a good sense of humor. That's just my unscientific opinion.

Room 47 is a black box theater. It's used for rehearsals and the occasional performance by some overly talented senior who does a one-woman show of Ruth Draper monologues that she uses to audition for the theater program at the University of North Carolina School of the Arts.

There are a bunch of upperclassmen sitting on painted black wooden cubes formed in a circle when we arrive. Diane Davis pops up and comes right over to me. "Our director of photography and set designer!" Diane says to the group, introducing me with the announcement of two jobs I've never done before. Great.

I settle on a cube and pull out my laptop. Diane starts the meeting by talking about a play that they do every year that was written about the founding of the Prefect Academy by a student who graduated in 1938. Diane explains that they, the committee, would like to breathe some life into the old script and come up with something new. She passes around photographs of past productions.

I've seen better theatrics at American Girl birthday parties in Manhattan. In the photos, the students romp around in bad wigs, long dresses with bustles, and high-top shoes made out of modern shoes with paper spats glued on top. Awful. The scenery is bad. Paper trees in one, and a giant map of the campus painted on a sheet in another. The worst.

"Something wrong, Viola?"

"Have you guys ever heard of blue screen?"

"What's that?" Diane asks.

"Well, I am able, with the proper technology of course, to take video I've shot and put it on a giant screen behind the action. Something like this."

I turn my laptop around and show them how I wrote my Shakespeare paper for Carleton's class with images I downloaded of Shakespeare's England and then wrote passages that appear at the bottom of the page explaining the action.

"We could have that onstage?" Trish's eyes widen.

"Yeah. I could film around campus and then you could do the play in front of the scenes."

"Oh my God. This is great." Diane sits up straighter on her cube. She is proud to change the course of crappy Founder's Day productions of the past and bring them into the new century.

"It'll take some work, but it could be pretty great," I admit.

"Could you work with Mr. Robinson in computer science? He helped install the computer tech system in the theater."

"Sure. Whatever works," I tell her.

* * *

When I get back to our quad, there's a bowl of cold microwave popcorn waiting for me on my desk. Marisol is asleep already. Suzanne and Romy are doing their homework by the small, bright beams of their desk lamps so as not to disturb Marisol.

I tiptoe to my desk and pull out my laptop.

"Sorry the popcorn is cold," Romy whispers.

"No problem," I tell her.

I IM Andrew.

Me: You up?

AB: Yep.

Me: Just got dragged into the Founder's Day—shoot me now—planning committee. I'm doing sets for the play. They didn't know anything about blue screen.

AB: No way.

Me: Yeah.

AB: Do you have the new program for it?

Me: There's a new one?

AB: Yeah. We used it on our fall production of All My Sons at LaGuardia.

Me: No way.

AB: You want it?

Me: Absolutely. I can already see this thing is gonna eat up, like, my entire life. The old program takes forever. I don't have time to program each individual scene.

AB: This will help. You download the images, and this actually sorts and stores them per your instructions. Then you just do an assembly on a DVD and you're done.

Me: That will save me hours!

AB: Okay. Will send.

Me: You rock.

AB: I know.

I sign off my computer, so tired that I think I may skip pajamas and BR (beauty routine). But I think of Mrs. Doughty and her false teeth, and how I'd like to grow old with my own choppers, and the only way for *that* to happen is to take care of them, so I grab my toiletry kit and head to the bathroom. Nothing like the idea of dentures to get me to brush, rinse, and floss before bed-time. First, though, I wash my face with Cetaphil. I dry it carefully, remembering that my mom told me if you scrub your face too hard it tears the fibers underneath, which leads to premature saggage, which I have to start thinking about when I'm thirty. But my mom says good habits can't start too early. My mom knows everything about skin maintenance, even though she totally skips steps when it comes to her hair.

I look in the mirror. I think my bangs grew a little

today. If I really yank, when they're wet I can almost get them to go behind my ears (almost). I really want them to be that long by the time we go to the dance at Drab Dull. That would be great.

I brush my teeth and think about Andrew and how, no matter what it is or when I call him, no matter what I need, he is *there*. I don't think any of my new friends here have someone like Andrew back home. They have friends, but not friends like *him*. I'm very lucky.

Caitlin used to tell me that there are no accidents in life—that people come into your circle because you have something to learn from them. I think about Suzanne who has definitely helped me be very cool about boys. Romy has encouraged me to be as athletic as is possible with my limited talents in that arena. And Marisol has been good for everything else—I can tell her anything and she never acts shocked or judge-y.

Even if I crash and burn academically here, and socially at Drab Dull, I *do* have the support of my room-mates. This is not a small thing for someone like me who spent the first part of the semester wishing I was anywhere but here. I'm beginning to understand that there is only now, and even though now isn't perfect, and South Bend isn't Brooklyn, that of all the billions of places I could be, this is what I've got right now. I've made three good friends, and hopefully I've become one for them too, and maybe that's what my mother meant when she said she never forgot her year at PA. Maybe it was the friendships that got her through—and is the part that she will always remember.

FIVE

FOUNDER'S DAY IS A MUCH BIGGER DEAL THAN I *EVER* thought it would be. It's more like Founder's Week. The rehearsals, filming the video for the show, editing the footage, adding music—the bells and whistles of production—well, all of it has eaten up most of the month of October, which is good, as the notion of time flying around here is one to embrace and celebrate.

My grandmother texts me to see how I'm liking school, as she was very worried that I wasn't adjusting. (My mother can never keep my emotional state to herself—not ever!)

Grand: How's the play going?
Me: You could never be in it.

Grand: Why not?

Me: You're too fine an actress. The girls around here are hams.

Grand: I can do ham.

Me: Please.

Grand: Do you need anything?

Me: The cookies were a hit. Thank you.

Grand: Fabulous!

Me: The food here can be sketchy.

Grand: That's true in all institutions.

Me: Good point.

Grand: I miss you, Viola.

Me: I miss you, too. I hung the picture of you as a geisha from *The Mikado* over my desk. Everybody thinks I'm half-Asian now.

Grand: That's marvelous!

Me: I know. Came in handy when I had to do a report on the San Francisco production of the Stewart Wallace opera *The Bonesetter's Daughter* by Amy Tan. Everybody thought I had some inside track on the China angle.

Grand: LOL.

Nerves are, like, totally out of control at the final dress rehearsal for the Founder's Day play called *The First Academy*. I am, seriously, the *only* person who is calm and refuses to freak out. That's because all my work is done and all I have to do is hit the cues and change the blue screen when the scenes change. Also, I have help.

Mr. Robinson is a true computer geek. Prefect Academy had a whole theatrical computerized light and sound system donated from a mega-rich alum (Trish told me), but no one has really used it to full effect. Until our show. Until now.

Mr. Robinson hooked up my laptop and the blue-screen program Andrew sent me to the main board in the mezzanine of the theater. My scenes look like, well, Broadway quality.

The play opens with some footage of the winding road that leads up to the academy. I shot it in early-morning light, and it's beautiful—lots of pink light—and I shot this cool effect (which I totally stole from *Saturday Night Fever*) where I follow the feet of the first student (Clare Brennan in character) to register in 1890. Then I widen out to show the first hall ever built.

The play proper stinks. The dialogue is stilted and the costumes are homemade. The upperclassmen wear uniforms from the past just like Mom remembered. Diane Davis wears a tennis outfit, white bloomers over the knee with a dress over it. Trish went for the gray serge jumper with the drop waist. It's actually as hilarious as it is educational.

But my scenery is amazing if I do say so myself. The

girls onstage can hardly give their lines as they look upstage at the skrim and my backdrops. Their jaws drop as the scene behind them changes from different points of view, to skylines, to day, to night.

Diane Davis shouts from the orchestra, "Viola! Can you hold the sunset over Geier-Kirshenbaum?"

I check my computer log and click on the image of Geier-Kirshenbaum. It appears onstage in full.

"Stunning!" Diane waves and gives me the okay sign.

"This program is really something," Mr. Robinson says as he sits back on his stool with wheels and folds his arms across his chest. He's bald and wears glasses, like every computer science teacher in the United States of America.

Romy, Marisol, and Suzanne sneak into the mezzanine from the exit door and sit in the back row. I turn around and wave.

"Cue the atrium shot," Diane directs.

I pull up the atrium shot of the girls on their way to class first thing in the morning.

"Wow!" Marisol blurts.

Diane covers her eyes and looks up into the spotlight. "This is a closed rehearsal!" she reminds us. Marisol covers her mouth and slinks down into her chair.

When the final dress rehearsal is over, Diane confers

with her actors onstage.

"I'd say the blue screen is the hit of the show," Mr. Robinson confides as he closes his laptop.

"Thanks for your help," I tell him.

"Nope, don't thank me. This is all you, Viola. And that program you bogarted out of Brooklyn."

"That made a difference," I agree. I'm really happy with how it turned out.

Romy, Suzanne, and Marisol come down the aisle to join me.

"That was amazing," Romy says.

"Sorry I shouted like that. It's just that the backdrop was so gorgeous," Marisol gushes.

"You knocked it out of the park," Suzanne agrees.

I look at my roommates who are so proud of me that it makes *me* proud.

"Group hug!" Marisol says. Suzanne and Romy swarm me with Marisol. This is the closest thing I will ever feel to having actual sisters. I'm so glad they came.

"Viola? Can you come down here please?" Diane calls from the orchestra.

"Gotta go. I'm getting notes," I tell them. Two weeks and I've already got theatrical lingo down. As I gather my stuff, my roommates turn to go. "Hey, guys."

They turn as one and look at me expectantly.

"Thanks for showing up. You're the best."

My roommates smile and I watch them push through the door of the mezzanine to the upper lobby. I feel, for the first time since I unpacked at PA, that I have a purpose. I'm *doing* something. Who knew that something would be a Founder's Day show? And who knew that the best audience would be my roommates?

I head back to Hojo after dinner to do a run-through of my computer images on the stage. It was hard to concentrate earlier when there were so many people around. Diane gave me my notes and there are a couple of adjustments I have to make. I wish Andrew were here to help me. We'd knock it out in no time.

I push open the door to the theater. The work lights are on, bright beams of white light that turn into murky gray pools when they hit the painted black floor of the stage. I walk down the side aisle and climb the steps to the stage. I turn and face the 300 seats in the theater. It scares me to stand here when the place is totally empty. I feel tiny, as though I'm standing on the ledge of the Grand Canyon. I don't know how actors do it. I admire Grand even more knowing she has to actually act on different stages all around the country in front of total strangers. She is very brave.

The scent of a flowery, powdery perfume fills the air. Theaters have a specific smell, a mix of wax, paint, and perfume that is worn either by the audience or the actresses—or maybe a mix of both. Whenever I went to the theater with Grand, I noticed the heavy perfume, and she said it was "the ghosts of drama past." I should've put that in my paper for Mrs. Carleton's English class. I bet I would have swung a B+ instead of a B–. Oh well.

I walk backstage into the wings and look over the racks of costumes. The characters' names dangle off the crook of the hangers. The costumes are pressed neatly in place and are organized by scene. The corresponding shoes rest in a neat row on the shelf above the rolling rack. On a table close by are wooden forms that hold the hats of each era, also arranged by scene. The hats smell like expensive perfume, roses, and honey. They're vintage hats with brims of velvet, satin bows, and fronds of feathers. Some have flounces of netting, others have hat pins made of rhinestones and pearls stuck into them. The work lights catch the facets of the rhinestones. They sparkle like the sun hitting the water in the fountain outside our room at dawn.

There's a table along the backstage wall, behind the skrim, marked with tape for the props from each scene. Putting on a play is a very methodical and organized process. I pick up a wooden ladle and a matching bucket, careful to place them back where I got them. After we do our show all of this will be put away, stored for another production. I'm a little sad to think I don't have an artistic venture planned after this one. And I wasn't counting on anything about lame Founder's Day being *this* much fun.

I pull out my video camera and begin filming the backstage area. I press Record and then Audio:

"The Viola Diaries continued. It would appear that I am showing you rows and rows of objects called props. They are. This is my first theatrical venture. The program calls me the set designer, though really I didn't do any of the crappy wooden chairs and tables you see in the scenes, but rather the high-tech visual landscapes that appear behind the actors as they play through their scenes. It's probably important to make note of this because someday, when I look back, it may signify the very moment where I set foot in the theater and stayed for a lifetime. Who knows? I can't be sure. I'm fourteen and it's pretty obvious to me that things change. But this is where I am today. At the Prefect Academy. South Bend, Indiana."

I sign off and lock in the date.

The theater has the scent of buttery wax and fresh paint. I go onstage and face the audience. I close my eyes and imagine a stage filled with ballerinas or World War I soldiers or a 1930s dinner party where ladies wore gowns. I open my eyes. I wonder if this feeling I'm having right now is "the bug." Grand always talks about when she was a girl and was bitten by the acting "bug"—as though it's a virus that races through you and once it does, you're never over it. And I think that might be true. Look at Grand. She's in her sixties and she's still got the "bug." I wonder if I've caught it too.

I look up and squint past the glare of the work lights. In the rafters over the stage, where complicated skeins of pulleys and ropes, wires and beams that lift scenery and hold lighting instruments in place live, I see a flash of red.

Whatever I'm seeing sort of freaks me out. I'm not one to stand still when I'm freaking, so I move quickly across the stage in rapid small steps like a geisha. When I get to the stairs that lead into the audience, I quicken my pace. I grab my laptop and my backpack off the lip of the stage and head up the aisle to go out into the lobby.

"It's only me," a voice says.

I turn slowly, afraid of what I'll see.

Mrs. Belldoin, the janitor, pushes her cart loaded with cleaning supplies through the stage door and onto the stage. When she sees me and the look on my face and the way I'm gripping my backpack like a pillow during a bad dream, she says, "Didn't mean to scare you."

"I'm okay."

"You know we lock the building at eight," she says.

"I know." But instead of heading out the door I get some courage, mostly because Mrs. Belldoin could take any guy in a fight, and there's nothing to fear when she's around. So I walk to the downstage lip of the stage and look up, up through the ropes, pulleys, and wires, past the work lights, and into the grid. The flash of red is gone—but not the scent of perfume. That stays.

> *Dear Viola,*
>
> *I called Aunt Naira about the possibility of the Red Lady following you around and spritzing places you go with her perfume. She said that ghosts don't, like, move around much. They stay in one building until they're chased out. So maybe you're not dealing with a normal spirit but something else. What, I don't know. She also recommended that you get your eyes checked. Flashes of red indicate something medical— like maybe the onset of myopia. At our age, that is very common.*
>
> *Tag Nachmanoff is dating two girls—Lucy Caruso and Maxine Neal. That's right, both at the same time.*

Not on the same dates of course, but neither are object-
ing. Can you imagine?

Love, Caitlin

(Oh, I might not be able to write back for a while.
My mom is looking for a new computer—this one is
acting up too much. It's so old it actually throws heat.
xoxox)

I can literally feel the admiration from my roommates when I enter the dining hall for breakfast the morning after our show. The Founder's Day show was a hit and it was a sellout crowd, mostly because every teacher in every class at PA made attendance mandatory for credit.

Some of the teachers who have been around here since the 1980s tell me it's the best Founder's Day they ever saw, and I got my own applause because Diane Davis made me stand up and take a bow during the curtain call. Now I'm sure I'll be hit up for every cam- era- and scenery-related project on campus. That's okay. I can always say no. And who knows, I might even say yes. I've never been treated this well. Trish made big comedy and tragedy masks for our quad door and trimmed them in glitter in honor of opening night. She made sure that I had a bunch of roses too. She's cool that way.

Mom and Dad video conference from Afghanistan:

"You guys look exhausted," I tell them.

"We are," Dad says.

"How's it going?"

"We're hanging in there. It's grueling," Mom says.

"We're on the move a lot," Dad explains.

"So come home," I say. "You're coming home in December anyhow, so just cut it short. Remember—you did that when you shot the documentary about street gangs in L.A."

"We've made a commitment and we're going to see it through," Dad says. "Besides, we've rented out the house until the end of your school year. The guy is nice enough to let us take it for two weeks over Christmas break; I don't want to push it."

My dad is always the font of practicality. "Okay, Dad."

"How are things going?" Mom leans forward. I can see in her eyes that she's afraid to ask.

"Good," I tell them.

Dad leans forward. "You're kidding."

"Nope. I'm totally blooming where I'm planted. And it's a complete freak accident."

"Honey, you know I don't like the words freak and accident together," Mom says.

"Sorry," I apologize cheerfully.

"We got the images you shot for the play. Your hand is steady and your eye is keen," Dad says proudly. "Must have been a great show."

"I guess I got a little bit of the theater bug, like Grand."

Mom and Dad look at each other, relieved. "I knew you'd find your place at the academy." Mom smiles. I like when my mother smiles. And I especially like it when *I* make her smile.

"It could all be ruined after the dance at Grabeel Sharpe Academy."

"That's where they got the boys for school dances when I went to PA." Her face lights up. "Oh, it's a lot of fun."

"Are they dorks over there?" I ask her.

"Well, it was 1983 and all of them had Rick Astley haircuts. There was one really cute guy. . . ."

"Hey," Dad says.

"Not as cute as you, honey. Anyhow, he looked like the lead singer from The Cars. And we were all after him."

"What happened?"

"He didn't go for any of us. But we had so much fun chasing him."

The thought of my mother chasing someone that looks like Ric Ocasek is too weird to think about.

"Oh, Viola, have fun!" Mom says. "You're going to have a ball."

"And behave yourself," Dad adds halfheartedly.

"I'm going to dress up and be a girl." I make a face that makes my parents laugh.

I can't sleep. I check the clock. It's quarter to three in the morning. I turn over, punch the pillow, and slam my eyes shut. I never had trouble sleeping in New York. I slept through sirens and all sorts of noise, but here in South Bend there's hardly any noise. Maybe that's part of my problem. I need noise.

I hear Suzanne sniffling in her bunk.

"Are you okay?" I whisper.

"Yeah." She blows her nose.

"Is something wrong?" I ask her. Sometimes Suzanne gets upset after she checks her email. I wonder if there's some awful boyfriend back home giving her heartache. She has never said she has a boyfriend, but what else could make a girl cry in the middle of the night: ninth-grade algebra? I don't think so. Plus, Suzanne is a math whiz, so it's definitely not *that*. "You can tell me if something's wrong." I turn and face her bunk in the dark.

After a while, Suzanne whispers, "There's nothing that can be done. And I'd rather not talk about it."

"Well, okay. But I'm having a hard time sleeping." I roll back onto my pillow and stare at the ceiling. "It's as if my mind is filled with clutter and I can't sort through it."

"You should go and see Mrs. Zidar," Suzanne whispers.

"Why?"

"She's good at sorting through stuff and maybe you have a medical problem."

"I didn't say I had a problem. I said I couldn't sleep."

"That *is* a problem. If you can't sleep most nights, something is bothering you and you should go and talk to someone who can help you find out."

"How about you?"

"Mrs. Zidar can't help me."

Silence settles over us, a deep quiet as dark as our room. Even somebody like Suzanne, who appears to have no problems, sometimes cries herself to sleep. You just never know. This is something that I've learned at PA that I would have never learned at home because I have my own room and I'm an only. Nobody has it easy, not even the Great and Tall Blond One.

Andrew and I have figured out a way to bring Caitlin into 2009 electronically, which is to *drag* her. Andrew had his mom call Mrs. Pullapilly and give permission for

Caitlin to come over after school and do a video conference with Andrew to talk to me. Finally she agreed, after we, like, begged the woman and Caitlin promised to do dishes for a hundred years and wash her dad's car on Saturdays. Insane! I wave at the video conference camera on my laptop.

"Hey, guys!"

"Your bangs are growing out!" Caitlin says, leaning into the camera on Andrew's computer.

"I know." I yank the bangs so they feather behind the tops of my ears.

"Hi, Viola!" Andrew squishes into the shot. He looks the same. Caitlin is wearing some kind of woven gold leather headband. Her black hair is blunt to her shoulders. Her dark eyes tilt up at the ends when she smiles, and it's great to see her smile. Her caramel skin looks beautiful year-round. She doesn't get that post-tan flakiness like non-Indian girls. Caitlin is fourteen, but if her mom let her wear lipstick (never) she would look eighteen easy with her full, perfectly shaped lips.

"What's the skinny?" I ask them.

"You go first."

"Well . . . ," I begin.

"Did you see the ghost again?" Caitlin asks.

"No. And I'm not sure it's a ghost anyhow."

"Okay, the mysterious red lady then. I wouldn't be afraid if I were you. My aunt Naira says only spiritually full people can experience visits from spirits from the other side."

"I ordered Tandoori chicken in honor of your ghost," Andrew jokes.

"I knew you'd figure out some way to make this about you," I tease him back.

"We can't wait for you to get home for Christmas," Caitlin says.

"I can't either."

"We're showing all our video projects on December twenty-second at the lab at LaGuardia." Andrew sits back in his chair. He looks a thousand miles away. "Can you make it?"

"Yeah. I'll be home by then!"

"Perfect," Caitlin says.

"Bring the ghost," Andrew says.

"I don't know if she travels."

"Aunt Naira is coming for New Year's—so you can ask her anything you need to know," Caitlin says helpfully.

The door slams behind me.

"Are you video conferencing again?" Suzanne asks.

"Yeah. Come over and meet Andrew and Caitlin." I

get up out of my desk chair. Suzanne slips in.

"Hi." Suzanne looks into the camera.

"Hi," Caitlin and Andrew say simultaneously.

"I'm Suzanne. I got the lower bunk because there was traffic on the Indiana Turnpike and I'm not happy about it."

"I can't believe you hold a grudge," I say jokingly.

Suzanne smiles up at me. "Uh-huh."

"It's nice to meet you, Suzanne," Caitlin says.

"I love your hairband," Suzanne tells her.

"I got it on the street," Caitlin says.

Boy, do I miss buying stuff on the street. Once I got a bag of six pairs of athletic knee socks with navy stripes for five bucks. I also got a lime-green faux patent-leather tote. I can only imagine the fashion season I'm missing on the corner of Mulberry and Prince. There's nothing like that in Indiana.

"It's cool." Suzanne nods in approval, then slips out of the chair. "Okay, I'm history. Bye, guys."

I slip back into my chair.

"She's nice," Caitlin says.

"I'm going to dinner." Suzanne grabs her coat and waves good-bye.

"Meet you over there," I tell her. Andrew hasn't said anything. "Andrew, are you okay?"

"She's a goddess," he says. (I told you Suzanne was gorgeous.)

Caitlin and I laugh. "Oh man. Suzanne is to Andrew like Tag Nachmanoff is to us."

Andrew is totally speechless. I'm almost embarrassed for him, but I'm also a little hurt—like she's the first pretty girl he's ever seen. Or is she? That doesn't say much about Caitlin and me, but oh well.

"I think I have to go now," Caitlin says. "Andrew?" She turns to him.

"Yeah. We gotta go."

Andrew and Caitlin sign off. As long as I live I will never forget the look on Andrew's face when he saw Suzanne on the screen. It was like one of those sci-fi movies where the sun gets really bright right before the spaceship lands. I mean, Andrew is not subtle at all. He has never admitted to even liking a girl before. And although he's my BFFAA until I die, he *is* a boy. I just never thought he was *that* kind of boy. I'm not the only person who's changed since starting the ninth grade, that's for sure.

SIX

MRS. ZIDAR'S OFFICE IS LOCATED OFF THE ATRIUM NEXT
to the All Faith Chapel, which I have yet to visit. The
famous "Hang in There, Baby" poster with the kitten
dangling by her front paws on a clothesline is taped to
her office door.

I unzip my camera from the case and make a slow pan
from the windows to the door in case I want to comment on this later. Then I turn the camera off and slip it
back into the case before my appointment begins.

To be fair, Mrs. Zidar found an office that is off on
its own and sort of perfect for privacy purposes. If
you're going to admit you need help, no need to make
an announcement to the entire student body by meeting with the school shrink in the main lobby. Besides, I

could be stopping in to see Mrs. Zidar for any reason—
like signing up for forensics (like, never), and no one
would necessarily guess I'm here for counseling.

The rest of the administrative offices are in Geier-
Kirshenbaum, which means even if you admit anything
of a horrible nature to Mrs. Zidar, it will take her some
time to run out her door and over to Headmistress
Grundman's and get you thrown out of school. As much
as I would love to go home, there is no home until my
parents return, so PA is still better than some reform
school in some small town in upstate New York. At least
at PA I've got my roommates. And even though Romy
totally blew my Saturday by making me sit in the stands
with Suzanne and Marisol while she played the longest
game of field hockey in the history of fields, I still like
them best, over everyone else I've met here. These are
the musings of my rational mind as I sit outside her
office and wait for my appointment.

I have noticed that since I made the appointment for
my mental health I spend a lot of time convincing myself
that I'm absolutely normal.

The only person I know who ever went to counseling
was Andrew's older brother, Gus, who became a little too
talented on the computer. He hacked into the LaGuardia
website and replaced the faces of the principal, vice

principal, and upperschool head with those of the Three Stooges. It was decided that there wasn't malicious intent, only a comedic one, so he didn't have to go to the therapist after a while.

"Come on in, Viola." Mrs. Zidar stands in the doorway of her office holding a clipboard. She wears a wool skirt and white blouse and Skechers leopard flats, for which she gets points. After all, she'd have to really hunt for those shoes in Indiana. It's not like they're sold everywhere. Or maybe she found them online. So, at least she's trying to be fashionable.

Mrs. Zidar's office is cozy, like a living room in a hunting lodge. The carpet is red and black and forest-green plaid. The sofa is covered in red corduroy, with two straight-backed chairs with red cushions on either side of it. Her desk is a farm table in front of the window with a rolling chair. There's an old jar filled with white carnations on the window ledge.

I sit down on the couch, which has such soft cushions I sink right in. Mrs. Zidar sits on one of the straight-backed chairs and scoots it to face me on the couch. "Make yourself at home."

I find it so odd when I hear the word *home*. It has a whole new meaning for me. It used to mean Hicks Street in Brooklyn, but now it's wherever I feel comfortable.

That's what boarding school does to a person who spent fourteen years of her life in one place—it has opened me up to new experiences and definitions.

"How are you, Viola?"

"I'm pretty good except I'm not sleeping very well. My roommate Suzanne said you might be able to help me."

"Are you a day bird or a night owl?"

"Either." I shrug.

Mrs. Zidar makes a note on her clipboard. "Are you eating well?"

"Except when they serve shepherd's pie. I'm not a fan."

"Okay. Do you exercise?"

"I take gym and dance."

"Do you like it?"

"Yep."

"Your physical filed with the school nurse says you're not on any medication."

"That is correct."

"So, how often do you have trouble getting to sleep?"

"Most nights."

"And have you always had trouble getting to sleep?"

"No, I always went right to sleep. I've had trouble since the Founder's Day show."

"Do you like your roommates?"

"Oh yeah. They're fine."

"And do you drink coffee?"

"Hate it."

"Cola drinks?"

"I like 7-Up."

"Chocolate?"

"Everybody likes chocolate."

Mrs. Zidar laughs. "That's true." She makes notes. "So what happened at PA that's keeping you up? Are you homesick? Are you worried about your grades?"

"I'm doing okay. No pink slips."

"Good. You know, you're quite the campus celebrity after the Founder's Day show. The upperclassmen were really impressed with your work."

"It was fun."

"So, it seems that on a health level, you're fine. You eat well, you exercise. You like your roommates, and you've found a way to be a part of the community that fulfills you."

"So, you're stumped?" I ask her.

Mrs. Zidar smiles. "Maybe you could tell me more."

"I'm going to be an artist. And I read a lot about artists," I begin.

"Go on."

"My parents are filmmakers, my grandmother is an

actress, so I'm sort of surrounded by creativity."

"That's wonderful."

"Well, it is and it isn't. I spend a lot of time in a land of make-believe, if you know what I mean. I imagine things. And I think that's how I got started imagining her."

"Her?"

"The ghost."

"You think you've seen a ghost?"

"Trust me. I've seen her."

"What does she look like?"

"Like an old movie star, except she's about twenty-five. And she wears a red dress and a black hat and shoes with buckles . . . of course, last time I thought I saw her, she was just a flash. I call her the Red Lady."

"Viola, have you ever heard of the subconscious mind?"

I shake my head.

"It's the engine that drives your imagination. It never sleeps. Did you ever take your camera out to film something, and you imagined what you were going to film and suddenly the light changes and you see in front of you what you saw in your mind?"

"All the time."

"Well, that is your subconscious mind."

"You mean I'm normal? Even though I'm seeing ghosts?"

Mrs. Zidar smiles. "You're becoming an artist. You're beginning to listen to the voice inside you and you want to interpret that voice. That's what artists do."

"I don't understand."

"You're not sleeping well because you're thinking about what you're going to create."

"You mean I'm putting a movie together in my mind?"

"The beginning of something. I don't know if it's a movie, but it's *something*." Mrs. Zidar looks at me. "I want you to think about what that means—and where inspiration comes from. You know, the place where art is born."

Quad 11, like every other quad that is filled with the seventy-five members of our freshman class, smells and feels like the main room at Super Cuts hair salon. I don't know how the power grid at PA will take it. We're all getting ready for the dance—blow-drying, hair-spraying, putting on makeup, and some of us, even ironing our outfits. The school buses are lined up outside like a row of yellow Smith Brothers' cough drops waiting to be filled with PA girls looking their party best.

Romy started at around four o'clock fussing with her outfits. She's changed, like, twenty-seven times. It's always the athletic girls who need the most time when prepping for a dance. This is not their comfort zone. They are most comfortable in uniforms, so they need extra time to put the right look together. Marisol tried a new hairdo for the dance (always a mistake). She used a flat iron to make her hair straight, and now she's crimping it with an iron (right there, a hole in the ozone layer with all the hair spray she has used tonight).

Suzanne breezed in from her shower and threw on, like . . . pencil-leg jeans and a white lace blouse and looks perfect.

I put down my blow-dryer. I brush my hair into place. My bangs are exactly two centimeters long enough to go behind the tops of my ears. This is a victory greater to me than acing my horticulture midterm. (No ho-hum results for me.)

The crimping is going to take Marisol right up to the time we have to board the bus and since I'm ready, I turn on my computer to check my mail. I IM Andrew, who I can see is signed on.

Me: I'm going to a dance tonight.
AB: Why?
Me: To dance.
AB: With guys?

Me: Yeah.

AB: Why would you go?

Me: Because my roommates are making me.

AB: Oh yeah. Right.

Me: It's not like I want to go. I have to. I'm being forced into being a team player.

AB: I get it.

Me: How's it going there?

AB: The same.

Me: Have you seen Tag Nachmanoff at school?

AB: Do you still like him?

Me: Yeah. But he's too old.

AB: Get in line. He's got, like, five girlfriends.

Me: Caitlin says two.

AB: Two or five—what's the diff?

Me: Right. Two or five or a million. It's impossible. Of course, if it were possible . . . maybe. But it's impossible and I don't try to achieve the impossible.

AB: Okay. Gotta go.

Me: Bye.

And the strangest thing happens—Andrew signs off. Totally signs off. He never totally signs off; he usually gives me a minute or two to think of additional information, a sort of instant message pause. But there is no grace period to add to our dialogue. He is gone. I turn off my computer, and sit, sort of stunned. "Okay, *that* was totally bizarre."

Marisol is dabbing Benetint blush on her cheeks. "What happened?" She smears in the rosy glow.

"Andrew was peevish about the dance. Sort of defensive."

"He's jealous," Suzanne says as she looks into her mirror.

"No way. We're BFFAA. We are *not* boyfriend and girlfriend."

"He may not know it yet but he'd like you to be his girlfriend," Suzanne says. "A boy doesn't hang around out of friendship."

"How do you know that? Is there a book or something?" I ask.

"If there is, I'd like to read it." Marisol pulls on her best jeans. They have leather laces on the sides of the legs. I think they're a little too cha-cha for our first dance, but what do I know? I'm in a Delia's jumper. I could be off the mark by two fashion cycles myself.

"It's common sense." Suzanne puts on mascara in front of her mirror. "My brothers are very practical about girls. They don't waste any time on ones that won't be potential girlfriends. And they only aim for ones who will say yes if they ask them out. This should tell you everything you need to know about boys. They only go after what they *know* they can get. We girls, on the other hand, aim really high. We take a leap, like that guy you told us about, Viola. . . ."

"Tag?"

"Yeah, Tag." Suzanne flips her head over and fluffs her hair from underneath. Then she stands up and every hair, I swear, falls perfectly into place. "Take that boy, Tag. He knows every girl likes him, so he gets to sit back and pick which girl, out of all the girls at your old school, he is going to ask out. If I were you, I would scratch him from your list."

"I can't scratch him off; he's like . . . my highest dream." Now I'm sorry I ever confided in these girls about TN.

"Rule number one about boys: Do not waste energy on what will not bring you results."

Romy sits down on Suzanne's bunk. She smoothes the tulle layers on her micromini party skirt that she wears over her best jeans. "I know that's true from science. Energy has to be fed from a source. If you don't feed the source, it dissipates entirely."

"Same is true of liking a boy. If you cut off the thoughts, if you stop pining, you're free to find a boy who is attainable."

"I can't give up Tag."

"Why not?"

"Well, he's like an A on a paper you worked really hard on. He's a trophy after you win the districts in field hockey. He's like Shia LaBeouf who walks among mortals in Brooklyn."

"He's a dream," Romy says.

"Yeah."

"Well, that's all fine, but he's not *here*," Suzanne says, making more sense than I'm willing to admit. I live in enough of a dream world as I long for Brooklyn, make movies, and keep a video diary.

I'd like a little reality to tell you the truth. Maybe I'll find some at Drab Dull.

As the bus pulls into the entrance of the Grabeel Sharpe Academy for Boys, you get an official military feeling. I had this reaction when visiting the historic battlefields near Waterford, Virginia, that my dad and mom dragged me through on a car trip so I might "understand the Civil War." The front gate is made of stone, with an enormous shield that says "GSA" in gold lettering and has a symbol that looks part eagle and part machine in the center.

The girls are laughing and having fun on the bus, and I have a feeling of impending doom in the pit of my stomach. If there's one thing I hate it's meeting new people in a large group, especially a group of boys.

I think it's sort of crazy to have to make friends at a new boarding school, and then haul us over to *another* boarding school to meet even *more* people—like, enough already. I'd be willing to go to a dance next semester, but now, in the heart of November, it seems way too soon. I've only adjusted to life at PA since, like, last Tuesday, and now it's all being shook up again.

It's not that I'm nervous. There are definitely girls on this bus who are nervous, who are made jittery by the idea of boys, but not me. Ever since the Founder's Day show, I feel very calm about who I am—as if I found a way to express myself that is truthful and very "me." It's the only way I can say it. I loved being creative and seeing my ideas realized in front of an audience. I'm not afraid of anything, not even boys. Awkward? Okay, maybe. But afraid? I have nothing to be afraid of. I know who I am. And if a boy doesn't like it? Well, too bad for him.

Mrs. Zidar stands up in the front of the bus and holds on to the silver pole next to the driver for balance. She's traded her mom jeans for a plaid wool skirt and navy blue twinset, which makes her look like a Scottish flight attendant. At least she has a good haircut and wears makeup. If Mrs. Carleton were our chaperone tonight, we'd have to be worried about what she'd wear. Mrs. Zidar, as a therapist, probably understands this and gussied up so as not to embarrass us. "Girls, a few words before we attend the dance. First, we are guests here at Grabeel Sharpe, so please, respect the physical buildings and landscape."

"Why doesn't she just say don't litter or write graffiti?" I whisper to Marisol.

"And remember your manners. Some of the freshman boys at Grabeel Sharpe may be a little shy, and it's up to us to make them feel at home."

I raise my hand. "They *are* at home; we are the intruders."

The girls on the bus laugh. Mrs. Zidar smiles. "Yes, Viola, that's true. But I know our Prefect girls, and you're warm and delightful and charming, and you are able to put everyone at ease. So why not tonight at your first dance?"

"Cool." I shrug. I may have a totally blasé attitude, but I'm having outfit remorse. This velvet jumper with the wide straps feels like a belted feed sack, which is very appropriate because lined up behind my classmates, I'm beginning to feel like I'm on my way to the slaughter.

My jean jacket, with an embroidered Juicy logo on the back (authentic), is not warm enough for the November chill. I have on black tights and dark blue suede ankle boots. My camera hangs around my neck, as I promised Mrs. Zidar and Trish I'd "record" the first dance for posterity. I'm relieved I have my camera with me; it gives me something to do. When all else fails, there's always art itself.

The foyer of Grabeel Sharpe smells like oats and Pine-Sol. They must have scrubbed the place before letting us off the bus. The interior walls are made of big blocks of gray stones, with giant brown crisscross beams on the white ceiling. It has the feeling of the outer lobby of a theater hosting a Renaissance fair.

On the walls are portraits of men who look like versions of Ralph Waldo Emerson and George Washington: oil portraits framed in ornate gold, the men wearing ruffly shirts with black jackets and stand-up collars. Drab Dull Academy deserves its nickname. The people who founded this place look stuffy and stern and boring.

"I hope they have good snacks," Marisol says as we follow the crowd.

"They will," Trish says from behind us.

"Like what?" I ask her. Trish looks pretty in a jean miniskirt with a billowy blouse, not unlike the ones worn by the founding fathers of GSA. She has her hair down and poofed out. You hardly notice her Invisaligns.

"Marisol and I like to eat more than dance."

"They'll have good stuff like sliders and French fries."

Marisol smiles. "My kind of party."

We follow Mrs. Zidar down the grand hallway through a set of wide doors that lead to the party room. The first thing I notice is that it's very cool in the room, as wide doors at the far side of the room are open to a large garden where there's a DJ set up. The room has tall windows on both sides, with long navy blue velvet curtains tied back with red braided cords. A series of dimly lit wrought-iron chandeliers hang overhead.

The food table is filled with good stuff, just like Trish promised: I see nachos and quesadillas and sliders and a giant tin of caramel popcorn. There's a tower of cupcakes by the punch bowl. Marisol's eyes widen when she sees the cupcakes.

Mrs. Zidar shakes the hand of a man who must be the GSA chaperone of the dance. They laugh like they've been through this a million times, which oddly enough, makes me feel better about the whole evening. The freshman dance has probably happened every year since 1890, which takes the pressure off.

Trish is greeted by some hot-looking upperclassmen who must know her from somewhere like resident advisor training. They flirt with her, which puts Trish in an entirely different category than I have had her in all these weeks. The guys don't seem to mind the braces, and when I look at Trish from a distance she looks pretty. I see why they like her; she's easygoing and fun.

Out on the patio, we see the clumps of freshman boys. They wear gray slacks and navy blue blazers with red-and-gray striped ties. I'll have to get a shot of Mrs. Zidar with them—as they look like pilots on the airline for which she wears plaid. Andrew will get a kick out of this back home. The entire concept of uniforms and mandatory dress codes is lost on him.

"Hi," a boy says from behind me. I turn around to see a tall boy with a nice face. He wears glasses and his bangs are long and pushed forward, but the back of his black hair is short. There must be rules here about haircuts. I look around. Most of the boys here have short hair; nobody has long hair like Andrew or Tag Nachmanoff.

"Hi," I reply, suddenly shy.

"What kind of camera is that?" he says.

"A Canon XH A1," I answer.

"Me too." He holds up the same camera hanging around his neck. "I'm Jared Spencer."

"I'm Viola Chesterton." I smile.

Behind Jared, Suzanne, Romy, and Marisol give me a

thumbs-up and head for the sliders. Now I have to talk to this new boy.

The first thing I notice about Jared is that he's massively cute (a good but prominent straight nose, nice lips, and long neck—necks are not something you notice unless one is absent—but his is nice). The second thing I notice is that he's comfortable. He doesn't seem rattled at all by this strangely formalish dance, or clumsy when it comes to meeting new people. It's all very natural to him, which puts me at ease. (I kind of can't believe it. A total surprise.)

"So, would you like something to drink?" Jared asks.

"Sure."

As we walk to the punch bowl, I can feel a bunch of eyes on us. And I don't mind it.

"What are you going to film tonight?" he asks.

"I was going to play it by ear, just have some fun with it."

"Me too. Have you made a film yet?"

"Not exactly. So far, I keep a video diary. My parents are doc makers."

"Really?"

"Yeah. They're in Afghanistan right now doing some work for a network news division. They're part of a team filming a movie about Afghan women."

"That's really cool." Jared smiles. He has a wide smile and good teeth. I wonder if he wore braces. It sure looks it. Jared pours a glass of punch and gives it to me. At the far end of the party room, I see Suzanne holding court, introducing Romy and Marisol to a group of boys. "Are those your roommates?"

"How did you know?"

"You came in together. That's pretty much the way it goes at boarding school—on field trips you stick with your posse."

I laugh. "A field trip?"

"Well, it's a dance—but to me, anyplace they take us on a bus is a field trip."

"Good point."

"Where are you from?"

"Brooklyn, New York."

"That's cool. I'm from Milwaukee."

"What are you doing here, at this school?"

"Every man in my dad's family went here. I didn't want to, but I didn't have a choice."

"Me either. I never wanted to come to boarding school and I sure didn't want to come to boarding school in Indiana. The good news is I only have one year of this and then my parents will be home and I can go back."

"A year isn't so bad," he says.

He's right. It's not the end of the world like it was back in September. Soon it will be Thanksgiving and then Christmas and I figure the spring will go quickly. "No, it's not."

Suzanne, Marisol, and Romy are now on the dance floor. Some guys join them—they actually seem like they're having fun.

"Would you like to dance?" Jared asks.

"I guess so."

As Jared and I set our cameras on a shelf that is filled with trophies, I think of Tag Nachmanoff. Whenever I imagined my first dance, he was always the boy who would take me in his arms and I would look up at him, and have to go up on tiptoe just to sort of make the waltzing work. And he would whirl me around the room effortlessly and I would follow, like a long silk scarf during an Isadora Duncan–style dance. I imagined this moment so many times that I feel a little disloyal dancing with Jared when it's been Tag all this time. But I have to get over it. I'm in Indiana, not Brooklyn, and Tag is juggling dances with Lucy and Maxine and wouldn't even have the time to squeeze me in anyhow.

Jared takes my hand, which seems a little weird but mostly polite. We join my friends on the dance floor and I introduce them over the music.

I glance around and see Mrs. Zidar standing with the GSA chaperone as they look on with approval. Our first freshman dance is already a success and so far nobody has spilled punch, spray painted the walls, or set the velvet curtains on fire.

As we dance, I look off beyond Jared to the fringe of the dance floor. Some of my classmates look bored, and others so uncomfortable this might as well be a trip to the dentist. I feel badly for them. I almost feel guilty having a good time, as if there's only so much happiness to go around, and it's just luck if you get a portion.

Marisol dances over and grabs my hand. Led by Suzanne and Romy, we make a ribbon through the crowded dance floor, almost running and laughing. Trish is chewing on a minipizza as she talks with an RA from GSA. She waves as we pass her.

Jared stands by waiting for me, laughing with the other boys. The dance we started went by the wayside when I joined my friends in this nutty conga line. I grab Jared's hand as we pass, and pretty soon all the guys on the dance floor have joined us. The DJ ramps up the music as we snake through the party room and out onto the terrace. I'm totally out of breath when Jared says, "Follow me. I want to show you something."

We go back into the party room and pick up our

cameras. I throw the camera strap over my head. It nestles around my neck comfortably. He does the same with his and I follow him outside. Normally, I might feel a little weird going off alone with someone I just met, specifically a boy, but somehow the cameras give us a purpose. We're two filmmakers, really, like my mom and dad who work together. Even though we've just met, my inner voice tells me he is totally cool. So I go with it.

Jared sits down on the low stone wall near the DJ's stand and flips his legs over the side. He extends his hand for me and I do the same. Once on the other side of the low wall, we head down a footpath with lowlights buried into the ground, lighting the way. I look back at the main building. I can hear the music and the laughter, and for real, the GS Academy looks like a castle.

"Check this out," Jared says. He motions for me to follow him in a sharp turn on the path.

Before us is a lake with an old rickety pier extending out to the center. A series of canoes lie on the shore like yellow matchsticks. The moon overhead pours silver light onto the lake, turning it a shimmering blue. The cold November wind ruffles the edges of the water. I can hear the soft shift of the moorings as the water laps against it.

"This is beautiful," I tell Jared. I flip the lens cap off

my camera and look through it. Just enough light to get some movement on the water. Jared slips off his lens cap and takes a different angle of what I'm filming.

"I come down here all the time," he says. "I was hoping the moon was bright enough for you to get some of the scenery tonight."

"It's just bright enough," I tell him. "This is really nice."

I focus on the light on the water, then widen out to take in more of the lake until it turns into black murk in the distance.

Jared stops filming before me and walks down to the edge of the pier. I follow him and we sit on the end and look out over the water.

"Milwaukee's pretty close to Indiana. Do you go home on weekends?"

"Not much. My dad and mom are divorced. My dad remarried and has a family. . . ."

"You could visit your mom, couldn't you?"

"She just got remarried too."

"Do you like your stepparents?"

"They're okay."

I don't know why, but I'm very interested in what Jared Spencer comes from. I don't want to sound like I'm prying, but I'm very comfortable with him. Maybe all those hours hanging out with the Bozelli brothers have made me a halfway decent conversationalist when it comes to boys. I'm not nervous at all. I want him to like me, I guess. And at the same time, I can tell that he does, and that makes me smile.

Jared looks out over the water. "What about your parents?"

"They've been together since college. I'm an only child."

"That's really cool."

"How many brothers and sisters do you have?"

"There's just me with my parents. And then my dad has two stepkids. And my mom is pregnant with a new baby."

"So you were an only child until they divorced."

"Yeah," he says. "I guess that means we have something else in common." Jared looks at me and smiles. "And all I've ever wanted is to live in New York City."

"Really?"

"It's where all the great filmmakers are trained. I read a lot about the USC film school, but I really like NYU. And then there are all the New York filmmakers like Darren Aronofsky, Nancy Savoca, Martin Scorsese, and Spike Lee. I admire them all a lot."

"So do I."

"Who inspires you?"

"Well, my parents are really great documentary film-makers. I love Albert and David Maysles and Constance Marks—she made this amazing documentary called *Green Chimneys*. My mom and dad are big fans. And Michael Patrick King, of course. They call him the King of Romantic Comedy."

I get up and stretch my legs. I'm feeling a little guilty that I promised to film the party, and I haven't shot one frame. "Have you ever made a movie?"

Jared stands up next to me. "A short subject. I did a story about an old lady in Milwaukee who decorates sugar cubes," he says.

"You're kidding."

"I know. It seemed like a dumb thing."

"I didn't mean that," I clarify. Boys can be sensitive too. They're just not known for it. "I meant it sounded interesting."

"It was. It started off about old-world craftsman-ship but became so much more. I interviewed her and watched what she does—she decorates the sugar cubes in miniature with tiny roses, or daisies, or letters, and then she boxes them and sells them."

"Mom and Dad always say that they start out thinking they're making one documentary, and then the subject dictates what the movie will actually be about once they start filming."

"That's exactly what happened to me! I had no idea that my movie would end up being about fleeing communism. I really thought it was about decorating sugar cubes. Have you ever seen them?"

"Yeah. My grandmother makes formal tea, and she uses them." How funny. I just realized that I call my grandmother Grand, and that she actually does grand things—like make tea and serve it in a silver tea service with decorated sugar cubes and miniature sandwiches. It's even more interesting to me that it's a boy I just met who helps me make that connection.

"What was compelling to me was the story behind the woman. How she brought the art form to the United States from Czechoslovakia after the uprising of 1968 when the communists took over. A Czech-American family in Milwaukee sponsored her, and she moved here and basically saved her life and the life of her family by making and selling the sugar cubes."

"I'd love to see it sometime."

"Sure. I can show it to you." Jared twists the lens cap on his camera without removing it. I do the same thing, sort of an involuntary cameraman thing.

"Maybe we should get back." I look up toward the

main hall of the academy. Although, if I'm really honest, I'd rather stay here and talk to Jared all night. But that's not an option. Trish and Mrs. Zidar would send out a search party.

I have a feeling that this is the beginning of something interesting with Jared Spencer. It's the first time in my life that I've met someone my age who is as passionate about making movies as I am. Most of my friends back in Brooklyn are good at lots of things, and I'm really only good at film. I can tell that's also true for Jared.

"I'm hungry," he says. "Are you?"

"Yeah," I admit. Here's more proof I'm comfortable with this new boy. I'd actually eat in front of him.

Caitlin Pullapilly says she doubts she'd ever be able to eat on a date in front of a guy she liked. I thought that was sort of dumb—people *have* to eat—and why wouldn't a girl eat in front of a boy? Caitlin says she'd be too nervous. But I'm not at all nervous with Jared, and I can't wait to tell Caitlin that when she finds a boy she has a lot in common with, she won't be anxious either.

Jared follows me back up the path. The moon is even brighter now, and I wish I could turn around and go back and film the water again. The perfectionist in me comes out when light changes to benefit my camera work. But Jared doesn't turn back, so I don't either.

Marisol is waiting for me by the DJ station. She looks relieved when she sees me. "Trish asked where you went," she says nervously.

"I went on a walk with Jared," I tell her.

Marisol's eyes widen at the news. "Well, at least you're back." Marisol follows Jared and me into the main room to the food table. The table is totally picked over and getting bare: the quesadillas are limp, the sliders have slid, and the popcorn is basically rubble at the bottom of the bowl, more kernels than puffs.

"Sorry," Jared says. "Looks like the food is gone."

"That's okay." I smile. "Let's make some movies."

Jared and I slip off our lens caps and work through the crowd. I spin and get the faces of the freshmen, increasing the shutter speed. Then I go out into the main hall and do the same with the oil portraits. When I return to the party room, Jared is interviewing some of the girls from PA, including my roommates.

"Did you know they call the girls of Prefect Academy 'Perfect Girls'?" he asks.

"Did you know they call Grabeel Sharpe . . . Drab Dull?" Romy says dramatically into the camera.

"That's cold." Jared laughs. "Do you think it's true? Having survived your first freshman dance?"

"I don't think it's drab and I don't think you're dull,"

133

Romy says flirtatiously, but with a wink to me. She twirls and the tulle layers on her skirt flounce out.

"But you did run out of cupcakes," Marisol says.

Jared turns the camera on her. "We'll make sure that we don't next time."

"Fair enough," Marisol says.

The DJ cranks up the music again and Jared introduces me to his roommates. They seem very nice, but I don't really pay much attention because I'm most interested in Jared. I can't believe he's exactly my age and he's already made a movie. That's pretty impressive.

Suzanne pulls me aside. "So . . ."

"So?"

"How's it going?" Suzanne says *going* like it's eight syllables long.

"Great."

"Fabulous," she says with satisfaction. "See, we're all still standing and we're all still alive."

"Girls, it's almost time to get back on the bus," Trish calls.

Suzanne goes to gather Marisol and Romy. I look around to say good-bye to Jared. I don't have to look far. He motions to me from the door. "Can I walk you out?" he asks.

"Sure."

Jared guides me through the hall to the front entrance

door and outside. It's about fifty degrees cooler than it was by the lake. A shiver goes up my spine.

"Are you cold?" he asks.

"It's like it turned into winter during the conga line."

"I know," he says with a laugh. I like his profile.

"And I wore this flimsy jacket." I pull it tightly around me.

"I like what you're wearing," he says.

"You do?"

"Yeah. You're very original. I like that. And you're pretty without being, I don't know, all made up."

If only Jared Spencer knew how long it took me to get this natural look. I used a pineapple face scrub, followed by Proactiv moisturizer, and then some Benefit Lemon Aid, and Tarte lip gloss. I may look natural to him, but only as natural as the makeup my mother actually allows me to wear.

I follow him down the sidewalk. His compliment gives me this strange and new confidence that I never had in Brooklyn. Even Tag Nachmanoff, with his total admiration of my computer and camera abilities, never made me feel like a beauty. I feel like a beauty around Jared Spencer and there's nothing wrong with that. It's like I'm at the beginning of a long marathon—going where, I don't know—but I like that I'm getting a running start as opposed to tripping and falling and lying there like a total disaster. Caitlin and I always talk about how it will be when we finally meet a boy who could be a potential BF. How will we know? Will there be signs? And I can't wait to tell her that it's just mutual, and sort of no fuss. My mom always says "you just know." And it's true. I like Jared, as much as I can after one school dance.

The last strains of music waft out of the doors of the Grabeel Sharpe building. The dance is over, but it's not a letdown. It was a success from what I can tell. A group of girls is laughing and talking with a group of boys by the bus. Mrs. Zidar is having a big laugh with the GSA sponsor. Girls continue to pour out the front door and onto the sidewalk.

Jared walks me across the crunchy gravel to the side of the dark bus. The driver is not on the bus yet. Jared looks around. When he sees that no one is nearby, he takes my hand, and then places his other hand on my face. The only place on my body that isn't shivering in the cold is where his warm hand meets my face. I close my eyes. I'm shaking from the night air.

"I had a great time tonight," he whispers.

"Me too," I tell him. I mean it.

And then Jared Spencer of Grabeel Sharpe Academy leans forward and kisses me. First, softly on my lips, and then once on each cheek, as if to cover my entire face with sunshine. He brushes his lips over my ears and says, "I hope to see you again sometime."

"Me too."

The gravel crunches under his loafers as he walks back to the entrance. I stand in the dark and watch him go. When he kissed me, the world sort of went silent, and now, it's as if it's bursting with noise, as though the volume has been turned to high. I hear laughter, and talking, and whistling in hi-def sound. The engine of the bus starts up with blaring intensity. The dizzy noise matches my dizzy feelings. Weird. Suzanne, Romy, and Marisol come running around the side of the bus.

"What happened?" Marisol asks.

"What do you mean, what happened? Didn't you see? He kissed her!" Suzanne says this triumphantly like I just won the gold medal in downhill skiing at the Winter Olympics or something. "It was so romantic."

Make that pairs figure skating, not downhill skiing. I want to say something, but I can't. I'm savoring the moment.

"This is so fabulously great!" Romy claps her hands together.

I nod, not wanting to say anything about Jared, or the lake, or the kiss. The kisses—three of them, not one—three! This is one of those times when explaining a feeling cannot measure up to actually having the feeling. And the best part? It's not for anybody else. It's just mine.

We climb onto the bus. I sit next to Marisol, while Suzanne and Romy sit in the seat behind us. Romy leans forward and she and Marisol give a blow-by-blow of the dance and the boys they met. Suzanne taps me on the shoulder and I turn around. She says, "Told ya."

I just smile back at her, then I turn and lean back in the seat. The chatter of the girls around me is like background music. I hardly notice it. I'm too busy thinking about Jared Spencer, which is about the best name for a boy I've ever heard.

I came to this dance tonight expecting the worst; I figured I would have a horrible time and go home wearing disappointment like the flimsy jean jacket I pull tightly around me to fend off the chill. Instead of something terrible happening, my whole life changed for the better. I went from fourteen, almost fifteen, totally unkissed, to fourteen, almost fifteen, totally kissed. Tonight, I am a Perfect Girl, because I had a perfect night. And it ended with three perfect kisses. Three. What a lucky number.

Of course, I can't sleep. I'm too excited from the dance, too excited about meeting Jared, and I'm starving. My stomach is actually growling. Suzanne, Romy, and

Marisol are asleep. Finally, looking for something to do, I get up and check my emails. There's one from Mom, another from Dad, two from Caitlin, two from Andrew, and one from . . . I can't believe it: Tag Nachmanoff! TN. (!!!!!) I open it.

LaGuardia sucks without the Riot. Nobody to fix my Avid. Keep the faith. Tag.

Before I print it out I put the font in calligraphy instead of American Typewriter Light because this is, like, historic or something that Tag thinks I deserve an email—a totally personal email. I can't believe he remembers me, and that school sucks without me. That means . . . he misses me. Now I'm practically sorry that I kissed Jared Spencer three times! How could this all happen in the same twenty-four-hour period? This is too much good stuff: a layer cake of joy, of possibility!

I turn off the computer. Either I'm shaking because the heat hasn't kicked on, or I'm hungry, or, I don't know, I just became a full-fledged teenager with an actual life, but the world has changed. I'm completely different. Maybe my father was right, that you have to shake up your world sometimes. You can't just stay in Brooklyn, even though it's cool, and it's just a subway stop from

Christopher Street in Greenwich Village—the coolest place on the planet. Sometimes wonderful things can happen in other parts of the world, like Indiana.

I saw a full moon over a pristine lake, and I met a boy and I didn't panic, and he kissed me three times, and I laughed and I had fun and I danced. In Indiana! After a bus ride! It doesn't seem possible. But I'm learning that good things happen to people like me, and maybe this is just the beginning of lots of good things—a happy chapter in my video diaries, in the story of my life, my real life: Viola in Reel Life.

I pull the blankets up over me and nestle down into my bed. I wouldn't want to be anywhere else in this moment. I'm content in my quad with three girls who are rooting for me, who seem to want my happiness more than I want my own. For the first time since I unpacked, the Prefect Academy for Girls Since 1890 is really and truly—and I'm not kidding, not one bit—home.

SEVEN

NOTHING, AND I MEAN *NOTHING*, MAKES A GIRL MORE popular at PA than kissing a boy at the freshman dance at GSA. OMG. Who knew? This is, like, double the Founder's Day admiration. Triple. Quadrillion. I'm on a whole different level at PA now. The upperclassmen sort of look at me as one of their own now, even though I was pigeonholed as an arty type who wore the wrong shoes on the first day of school. I may even be able to wear my yellow patent leather flats again, because it's not so much about the shoes as it is about the person wearing them.

I went from rule breaker to rule maker overnight. No longer fringe, I am now mainstream. I thought academic achievement, excellence in field hockey, or not screaming in terror during mouse college in biology qualified for respect. But no. It's *dating.* That's the ticket to instant status at PA.

Andrew IMs me.

AB: *How was the dance?*

Me: I thought it would suck, but it was fun.

AB: *Were the guys in military uniforms?*

Me: Most of them just wore blazers and ties. And they aren't allowed to have long hair.

AB: *Bummer.*

Me: You'd hate it.

AB: *So, what did you do?*

Me: Had fun.

AB: *I took Olivia Olson to the movies.*

Okay, this is weird. I sit back in my seat. I meet a boy and suddenly at the very same moment, Andrew decides to date Olivia Olson? It can't be something in the water, as we are, like, three states apart. What is it?

AB: *Are you there?*

Me: Yeah, yeah. Sorry, Suzanne just interrupted me.

That's a lie. She didn't. She's in her bunk listening to

her iPod. I'm in a state of shock but I can't share that with Andrew.

AB: Olivia is not annoying anymore. I don't know what happened to her. But since her grandmother died, she's actually okay.
Me: Cool.

Olivia Olson is probably the best-looking girl in the ninth-grade class at LaGuardia. She's of actual and authentic Nordic descent so she is tall and blond and fierce in basketball. Nobody needs to make excuses for Olivia. She's not annoying; she's just a take-charge girl. A leader.

AB: She and I were put on a team for the science fair, and I felt I had to ask her out.
Me: Great.

But I'm thinking it's anything but "great." Andrew has to make it seem like he doesn't like her. I am sensing some insecurity and fear here. Maybe he's afraid she'll drop him.

AB: I hope you don't mind.

Me: Mind what?

AB: That I asked her out.

Why would he think I would mind? Even though I sort of do.

Instead of reassuring him, I tell him my news.

Me: I met a nice guy at the GSA dance.

I call it GSA instead of Drab Dull just to make the point that it wasn't *drab* or *dull*, it was *fun*.

Andrew doesn't respond for a moment. I bet he thinks I'm making Jared up just to be competitive. Okay. Whatever.

Me: Are you there?

AB: My mom called me.

Me: Do you need to go?

AB: Nope. So, who is this guy?

Me: His name is Jared. He's already made a movie.

AB: No way!

Me: Yep. Short-subject doc.

AB: Not full length?

Me: Nope.

AB: Okay.

Me: Okay what?

AB: Okay he hasn't made a full-length movie yet.

Me: Should he have?

AB: Not necessarily . . . Gotta go.

Me: Me too.

I don't know why I didn't tell Andrew *everything* about Jared. I guess when he said he was dating Olivia Olson, I didn't want to make it seem like I was competing with him. Andrew is my BFFAA, and not someone I have to impress. I'll leave that kind of silly competition to girls who need their guy friends to worship them. I like my friendship with Andrew to be pure.

The computer dings softly. I look up at the screen. OMG. It's Jared!

JS: Hi, Vi.

Me: Hi, Jared.

JS: What are you doing?

Me: Wishing I didn't have to research nuclear fusion in the twenty-first century.

JS: Boring.

Me: Tell me about it.

JS: I've been thinking about the pier.

Me: Me too.

145

JS: You're different.

Me: Thanks. I'd rather focus on the fact that you said I was pretty.

JS: YOU ARE.

Me: I like the caps.

JS: I figured you would.

Me: So what's new over there?

JS: Are you making a film for the Midwest Secondary School Film Competition?

Me: Don't know anything about it.

JS: I'll send you an application. It's for the spring. March deadline.

Me: Cool.

JS: I have to go home this weekend.

Me: Wish I could. Good for you.

JS: Is it? My mom is having the baby. C-section.

Me: Very exciting.

JS: Yeah.

I sit and think for a moment before typing. Then I hit the keys:

Me: I know that you're apprehensive about the new baby, but take it from me, if you stay open to new experiences, sometimes life works out in ways you least expect.

146

There is a pause before Jared writes back. Finally:

JS: *Thanks. You're sweet.*

I take a deep breath and type:

Me: So are you.
JS: *I hope to see you real soon. There isn't another dance until the new year.*
Me: Sign up for the lecture series.
JS: *Really?*
Me: We invite you guys to the lecture series.
JS: *Cool. I will.*
Me: Great.
JS: *It's a date.*

I take another deep breath before typing this, as my fingers are literally shaking with excitement. A date. How I love that word *date.* I type:

Me: It's a date.

Suzanne stands behind me. "Wow. That IM was about four miles long."

"I know."

147

"He really likes you," Suzanne says. "Excellent."

"You think?"

"I would say you are right on schedule." Suzanne flips her hair back into her hairband and it falls away from her face like gold ribbons.

"For what exactly?" I'm dying to know.

"Your first official boyfriend." Suzanne shrugs. "I mean, you do have Andrew back home, but that's platonic."

"Right."

"And that guy, Tag, he's a total fantasy, right?"

"I guess." I hate to admit it, but Suzanne is right. Only if there was some blight in Brooklyn that forced every teenage girl there to move out of the borough and I were the only girl left, then, and only then, would I have a realistic shot at TN. There's nothing wrong with that, it just happens to be true.

"So this is perfect." Suzanne stretches out on her bunk. "Sure makes life more interesting, doesn't it?"

I smile. It is perfect. Jared is *perfect* for me. I didn't think of him in that way, but it's true. He's just right.

Marisol and Romy come in carrying their books from math lab. The blue streaks in Romy's hair have grown out since we've been here and now they look like two blue feathers. I think her hair grows faster than the general population's and for sure, faster than mine.

"What a day." Marisol plops down on her bed.

148

"Is it me, or are the classes, like, getting so difficult you have to be Madame Curie to pass?" Romy unloads her book bag.

"You guys need a break," Suzanne says. "Listen, I asked my mom if I could invite you all home for Thanksgiving. She said, bring the quad!"

"Really?" Romy's eyes widen. "Are your hot college brothers going to be there?"

"Yep."

"Oh, I am *so* there." Romy laughs.

"Thank you. I'd love to go," Marisol says. "No way can my parents afford to bring me home at Thanksgiving and then again at Christmas."

"I know." Suzanne smiles. "Not that I eavesdrop on your phone calls or anything."

"I'd love to come," I tell Suzanne. "They keep school open, but we'll be stuck doing morning hikes with Mrs. Zidar—and pressed turkey in the cafeteria might kill me."

"Great. I'll tell my mom. We'll take the train into the city."

My appointments with Mrs. Zidar have become a pain. I really don't have any extra time to hang out and speculate about the roots of my insomnia when I have bio, horticulture, and English midterms that count for 30 percent of the grades in each class. I don't even notice how much I'm sleeping—or not sleeping—because I'm so busy.

"I sense you're getting a little impatient with this process," Mrs. Zidar says.

Oh, really, what was your first clue? I want to retort, but instead, I say, "No, I just have a lot on my mind." I'm dying to spice up these sessions with a play-by-play of the dance, my three kisses, and my obvious boost upward on the PA social ladder. But that's *way* too private.

"We could suspend our sessions until after Thanksgiving," she offers.

"Fantastic!" I stand up so fast it takes Mrs. Zidar aback.

"Well, that was easy," she says. "What are you doing for Thanksgiving break?"

"I'm going to Chicago with my roommates, all of us, to Suzanne Santry's."

"Wonderful!"

"I'll miss you on the nature hike," I tell her. "But I won't miss the pressed turkey with the yellow gravy."

Mrs. Zidar tries not to laugh.

Romy, Marisol, Suzanne, and I stand on the platform of Union Station after having made, like, a million stops between South Bend and downtown Chicago. I didn't mind all the stops because I knew at the end of the ride, I'd be back in a major city.

As I breathe in the Chicago air for the first time, cold and smoky with exhaust, I remember what I left behind in Brooklyn: sirens, traffic noise, and crowds. It's so peaceful in South Bend that I've actually forgotten how to tune out because there's no need to in a small city that folds up at nightfall. The only noise you hear in South Bend is the occasional long-distance fire whistle or the marching band at the University of Notre Dame when they practice their drills outdoors. I've missed the racket of city life.

Chicago is a sprawling city spread over miles, with a giant lake in the center, whereas New York City is crammed onto one small island. Chicago has skyscrapers like New York City, but here, there seems to be more room on the ground. There are wide streets and sidewalks. No cobblestones.

The sky over Chicago is expansive. At home, we appreciate the smallest stretches of sky. Sometimes a cloud that passes through what looks like a small blanket of blue between two buildings is all you will see of the greater universe.

"Crepes!"

Suzanne turns. "Kevin!" She waves. "Over here!"

One of Suzanne's brothers, Kevin, stands by the driver door of an old station wagon across from Union Station. He has layered light-brown hair and blue eyes. He looks even better in person than he did in the picture on Suzanne's desk.

Suzanne leads us across the median. Kevin grabs her duffel and mine and takes them around to the back of the car. Romy sort of freezes until Kevin smiles at her and grabs her bag out of her hands before throwing it in the back. Marisol stuffs hers in on top of the rest. "Step on it, girls. I'm in a tow zone."

We pile into the car. Kevin and Suzanne get in the front. Romy, Marisol, and I climb into the backseat. In the reflection of the rearview mirror, I see that Kevin has a nice smile and an overbite that has been partially corrected. He's major handsome. He looks a lot like Suzanne, with the same high forehead and strong jawline.

"This is Kevin," Suzanne says, giving her brother a big hug. "He's my favorite brother."

"Until Joe picks her up."

"He's your other brother?" Romy pipes up.

"Yep. But this is the one who counts, until I get my license of course."

"I'm not teaching you how to drive, Crepes," Kevin says, and he sort of twinkles.

"Why do you call her Crepes?" Romy asks. I think she couldn't care less about Suzanne's nickname; she just wants to keep the conversation going with Kevin.

"For Suzette. Crepe Suzette. Because she's so sweet," Kevin says.

"I'm going to be sick," I joke.

The drive to Lake Forest is speedy, as Kevin knows the back roads and the best ways to avoid traffic. He plays the radio loudly and, every once in a while, lowers the volume to say something to his sister.

We can only see the back of his head and occasionally his blue eyes in the rearview, but it doesn't matter. I can tell Romy is already crazy about Kevin. She applies pink gloss on her lips repeatedly until it's so thick, I finally lean over and whisper, "You look great." Romy has one of those instant love-at-first-sight crushes that almost-fifteen-year-old-girls *only* get on older guys. It's like Romy's been hit with a rubber mallet that we use to pound chicken fillets in healthy cooking class.

Romy leans forward from the backseat and asks Kevin a ton of questions about college. I think she likes that she has her face close to his and can check how they look together in the rearview. She asks him perfectly intelligent questions and Kevin doesn't seem to mind answering them. It turns out he's a freshman at Marquette University and he plays hockey. Partial scholarship. With that, he and Romy go into sports world with a conversation that only the athletically inclined would find remotely interesting.

Kevin pulls into the driveway of their house on a pretty, tree-lined street with sidewalks. The Santrys live in a cottage-style stone house with a black wrought-iron gate. Classy. The trees have a few golden leaves hanging on, but the ground is clear where they've raked. The yards are soft brown where there was once green grass. A large silk flag with a turkey embroidered on it hangs over the Santrys' entrance door. We grab our duffels and follow Kevin up the walkway.

"Ma, we're here. I got the kids," he says as we enter the house. Marisol and I look at each other. We can hardly be called *kids* after we've left home and lived on our own. We look over at Romy, who gets a look of concern on her face. She doesn't want her crush to consider her a *kid*. Her determined chin softens, but then she gets a steely look in her eye. I've seen this look when she plays field hockey and is strategizing her path to the goal. She's going to prove to Kevin she's not a kid but a young woman. Her work is cut out for her over this break.

The Santry house smells like cookies are baking in the oven (maybe they are). The living room is big and comfortable with large bright paintings and lots of books in stacks everywhere. There's an upright piano and potted plants in the windows.

Suzanne's mother comes out of the kitchen. She's wearing business clothes, and over them a faded apron that says FOR THIS I SPENT FOUR YEARS IN COLLEGE? "You made it!" Mrs. Santry greets us one at a time and gives us each a hug, which makes me feel welcome and miss my own mother. We follow her into the kitchen. It's a bright yellow country kitchen with a blue tile floor and pots hanging over the sink. There's a large bay window overlooking a backyard with an above-ground swimming pool in the center of it.

"Come on over and meet my dad," Suzanne says.

I'm expecting a tall man (everybody in the Santry family is a giant) from the picture. We follow her to the bay window where her dad is sitting, reading. When we get close, I pause. Mr. Santry isn't sitting in one of the kitchen chairs; he's in a wheelchair. It's rolled up to the table. His feet are placed on the floor, not in the stirrups.

Romy looks at me, then at Marisol. We're all confused. Her dad must have been in an accident, but why wouldn't Suzanne have mentioned it?

Suzanne runs to her father and sits on his lap.

"Whoa," he says and laughs. Mr. Santry is as handsome as Kevin, and looks tall too. Suzanne takes her father's hand, which he cannot seem to lift. She gives him a kiss on each cheek and then hugs him tightly. "Who did you drag home this time?" He grins at us.

Romy, Marisol, and I look at one another. And then I laugh, and they follow suit. "We're spongers," I tell him. "Boarding school girls with no place to go on the holiday."

"But there's no place else we'd rather be," Romy says earnestly, looking at Kevin.

"Well, welcome to our house," Mr. Santry says and smiles.

"You should feel sorry for us," I tell him. "We're all alone in the world."

"Not anymore," Kevin says. I notice this comment makes Romy stand taller and smooth the last bits of the blue streaks in her hair.

"Why don't you girls go upstairs and put your things away? We have big plans this afternoon," Mrs. Santry says.

"Great." Suzanne climbs out of her father's lap and gives him another kiss. We follow her into the hallway. I turn and look back at Mr. Santry, who smiles at us. Mrs.

Santry goes to him and tucks the throw that rests on his legs. She leans down and kisses him on his cheek.

I follow Suzanne and the girls up the front stairs. The house feels like a country inn, with flowery prints and distressed furniture painted colors like cobalt blue and antique white. The artwork is fun, and framed photographs line the stairwell. The pictures are in rough-hewn frames from when the Santrys were children. Romy lingers on pictures of Kevin when he was young. I jab her with my elbow to keep her moving up.

"Okay, here's my room." Suzanne pushes the door open to a sunny and huge bedroom, painted with lavender and white stripes, and with a set of bunk beds and a trundle underneath. "You guys take the bunk and trundle."

"Where are you going to sleep?" I ask her.

"The trusty air mattress. Don't worry. I like it."

Romy, Marisol, and I set about placing our duffels next to our beds. It's so funny to have our quad transported intact from South Bend to Chicago. We are actually pretty good at moving as a unit.

"The bathroom is across the hall," she says. "Girls only."

"Too bad. I think Romy was hoping to share with Kevin," I joke.

"Viola! Am I that obvious?" she says.

"Not as obvious as that lip gloss."

"Seriously?"

"See what happens when a girl likes a boy? Her sense of humor goes right out the window," I say. Marisol and Suzanne laugh.

I find a plug and commence recharging my phone. Jared promised to text me later and I want to make sure my battery doesn't die. Suzanne checks her BlackBerry while Marisol and Romy check theirs. I can't stand it another second, so finally I say, "Suzanne, why is your dad in a wheelchair?"

"I'm sorry I didn't say anything before," Suzanne says with a sigh.

"You can tell us anything." Marisol sits down next to Suzanne on the bed.

"I know."

"What happened?" Romy asks softly.

"He has MS. You know, multiple sclerosis. And he was fine for a long time, and just in the last year it's gotten really bad. He can't walk now."

Romy, with her many parents, and Marisol with hers, and me with mine—well, we don't have this kind of problem. And to be honest, I don't think about it much. My parents are healthy and Grand seems even younger than my own mom.

Now I understand why Suzanne cries at night. She has terrible sadness, and probably worries about her father getting worse. "I'm sorry, Suzanne."

"It's okay."

"No, it's a lot to deal with," Marisol says. "You're away at school and it must be really hard to be away from him."

"I didn't want to go to PA. I wanted to stay here. But it was always in the plan and my dad insisted. He wants all of us to be completely normal—and that includes ignoring him sometimes and disobeying his rules. He said there is no room for perfection in the Santry house."

"Why didn't you tell us?"

Suzanne looks away. Her eyes fill with tears. "I don't know. I guess I thought that if I didn't talk about it, if I didn't say he's sick, maybe he won't be. That maybe I just dreamed the whole thing up."

"I get it," Marisol says. "You don't want it to be real."

Mrs. Santry knocks lightly on the door. "Everything okay?"

"Yeah. Oh yeah," Romy and I chirp.

"I heard you girls wanted to go to the Art Institute."

"We would love it," Marisol says.

"Freshen up and meet me downstairs."

We unpack quickly, placing our clothes neatly in empty drawers in Suzanne's dresser, then toss the big, empty duffels in the closet. We grab our purses and throw them over our shoulders.

Before we leave the room, Marisol gives Suzanne a hug. Romy looks at me and I look at her, and we go to Suzanne and Marisol and throw our arms around them.

"Okay, okay, I feel the love." Suzanne's misty tears turn to laughter. We all laugh.

"Now, if only Romy could feel the love of Kevin. That would make for the best Thanksgiving," I tease.

"I am totally gonna ratchet down my desire," Romy promises. But I doubt it. She's laying on more lip gloss as we go.

The Art Institute of Chicago is near Grant Park. It's a grand building, and while it doesn't seem as big as the Met in New York City, it surely is as wonderful. The greatest painters are represented here in the permanent collection: Georges-Pierre Seurat, Edward Hopper, Vincent Van Gogh, and Claude Monet. And these artists are just for starters!

Marisol wants to see some modern works. A favorite artist of hers is the late New Yorker Margo Hoff, known for her enormous and whimsical collages.

I don't really have anything specific in mind to see, I just want to soak up city life and mill around hordes of people wearing headsets. I want to be on the move, banging into people without saying "excuse me," see new and interesting things, love or hate those new and interesting things, take in art, talk about it! This museum trip will be the closest thing to being in New York City that I've had since the school year began. I hope I get shoved and pushed and cursed at, then I'll really feel part of things!

Mrs. Santry gives each of us a small metallic admissions button to clip onto our collars. "Okay, girls, you have two hours. Meet me back here at four thirty."

"Hey, look." Marisol hands me a brochure. "There's an installation on old movies."

I flip through a series of old black-and-white photographs from the 1920s. The title of the show is *The Roaring Twenties on Celluloid*. My mom and dad would love this. They took me to NYU last summer to see *The Birth of a Nation* on the big screen.

"How great." I'm thinking I can buy Jared a set of postcards or even a T-shirt. No, T-shirt says *going steady*, while a set of postcards says *three kisses by the bus*. I can't believe it: I'm already getting the hang of dealing with boys! I can thank Suzanne for that; she's the voice of reason when it comes to them since she's been dealing with them all of her life. Sometimes I wish I had a brother to talk to.

"I'm going through the permanent collection," Marisol says. "For the fundamentals. And then I'm going to check out the moderns."

"I've seen the moderns a billion times," Suzanne says. "But I'll go with you. A billion and one."

"I'm going to the sculpture garden," Romy says.

"Great. And I'm going to meet an old friend of mine in the cafeteria for a cup of coffee." Mrs. Santry smiles. She really is very pretty and she's gone out of her way to make us feel at home. When we left, Mr. Santry was watching football with Kevin, so we didn't feel bad leaving him behind. Mrs. Santry seems happier, lighter, being out of the house for a while.

"I'm going to the old movie exposition," I tell them.

"I went last week. You will love it!" Mrs. Santry promises.

"See you guys later." I walk toward the pavilion housing the old movie show. As much as I like hanging with the girls and living in our quad, sometimes I miss being an only child where I can set the agenda alone. I liked when I didn't have to consult a group. I liked when I could read late into the night with the light on and nobody would wake up and ask me to turn it off.

I liked lazy Saturdays where I'd read a little, then play on the computer, fix a sandwich, and eat half, or listen to music really loud. Although living with the girls has made me less selfish, I'm still going to savor being alone in the Art Institute.

I unravel my headset as I walk, looping it around my neck. It's so relaxing to be in a large crowd where nobody knows me; I don't even mind waiting on the long line into the exposition. I listen to the audio commentary.

A woman's deep and honeyed voice on the CD says, "Welcome to the Art Institute of Chicago. We are proud to present the traveling exhibition, *The Roaring Twenties on Celluloid,* in conjunction with the Los Angeles County Museum of Art. Enjoy the show!" Kicky flapper music ensues.

I move through cubicles filled with black-and-white photographs shot by a set photographer. Images of Rudolph Valentino fill one wall, the center of which is a virtual silver screen that runs images of *The Sheik* in rehearsal. A movie about making movies—how perfect.

The Rudolph Valentino section is filled with a tourist group of Italians who are led by a woman carrying a red, white, and green flag. There is hushed awe as they listen to the guide talk about Valentino's artistry.

I turn the corner and speed through the CD to get to

Our Own, a display about Midwestern talent in front of and behind the camera.

I peer into dioramas of set models from actual films. Then I turn and face a large wall with a slideshow of faces. The images flip through: actors with slick hair, pale, white powdered skin, and straight teeth with spaces between them; then images of actresses, platinum blond with bobbed hair and pencil-thin eyebrows.

I recognize a very young Joan Crawford from *Our Dancing Daughters*. She's a little chubby yet exuberant in her first feature film. The biography card to the side says that Joan lived in Missouri and attended Stephens College. Who knew?

I move to the next section, which says *Talent from Central U.S.A.* Here, life-size cutouts of actors and actresses in black-and-white grace a virtual set. There's a grouping of smiling women in drop-waist dresses wearing satin shoes tied with enormous ribbons. They have gorgeous multiple strands of pearls around their necks. One of the ladies drinks gin out of her shoe. I move along the exhibit, taking in the Roaring Twenties, an era of parties and more parties.

In an instant when I turn the corner, the display turns to Technicolor. As my eye settles on the platforms full of images bursting with color, I see a lady in red.

The image of the lady is pure Hollywood glamour. She is propped against a box, smoking. She wears a vivid, red, drop-waist dress. She has matching red shoes, dressy, with a square heel tied with red satin ribbons. Her blond curls peek out of a small black cloche hat. She looks directly into the camera through the mysterious haze of her cigarette smoke.

I stand back and squint.

I know her.

I have seen her.

OMG. She's the Red Lady from my video diaries. It's *her*. A feeling of complete anxiety grips me and I look around for someplace to sit down. A small bench in front of the display is empty. I go to the seat and look up at the Red Lady, to study her. To make *sure*.

I read the biography cards under the life-size photograph.

May McGlynn born in Winnetka, Illinois, October 11, 1900, was a favorite go-to comedic actress for writers Frances Marion and Anita Loos. The starlet was destined for great roles in the American cinema when her life was tragically cut short in an airplane crash in South Bend, Indiana, on September 3, 1925, days shy of her twenty-fifth birthday.

She died in South Bend, Indiana! Where?

I continue reading.

Her plane dropped from the sky and into a cornfield, part of the Prefect Academy, a boarding school for girls.

I don't know whether to be relieved or terrified—or both. So I continue to read to understand this May McGlynn.

A true flapper, a good-time gal, and a lush, according to reports, Ms. McGlynn personified the era of good feelings and scanty morals that was the 1920s. Ms. McGlynn was featured in chorus roles until her breakthrough film, Wilderness Cry, *where she proved her mettle as a dramatic actress.*

I pull the headset off my ears and stand. I look up at May McGlynn, *my* May McGlynn, *the Red Lady,* who is as real to me now as my own camera, in my own hands. She was real—she lived!

I didn't make up the ghost. What I saw *was* May McGlynn. She lives on reels in canisters in the basement of the Art Institute of Chicago, and when she's not on film, she's at the Prefect Academy trying to tell me something. But what exactly?

Now I wish that I had Marisol with me. Or Romy. Or Suzanne. Or even Mrs. Santry who I just met, but who seemed empathetic. This is a very bad time to be alone. My hands begin to shake.

I look up at May. The expression in her eyes comforts me. I search the crowd as it moves slowly through the exhibit, but I don't see her here. No one in red. No one in a hat. No one with those cool shoes. And for sure no cigarettes. A couple stops and reads May's bio on the display.

Looking at May is like looking at the photographs my roommates and I keep on our desks of people we know and love and miss. Just seeing the images brings connection.

Maybe this is what Mrs. Zidar meant; maybe May is real to me because I need her to be. After all, she was *in* movies, and I *make* them. That's what Dr. Fandu in horticulture calls a "symbiotic" relationship. And everybody knows that when there's a symbiotic relationship, something is born of that. I just have to figure out what that might be.

EIGHT

ROMY, SUZANNE, AND MARISOL ARE EATING CUPCAKES
at the museum café as though nothing has happened. I
run to their table and Romy looks up at me.

"What's wrong?" she asks.

"You guys. You have to come with me. Right now."

"Why?" Marisol looks concerned but continues to eat
her cupcake.

"I wanted to tell you guys but I was afraid you'd think
I was nuts."

"Tell us what?" Suzanne adds Splenda to her iced tea
as though this were the most normal moment in the
world.

"I was filming my video diaries the first day of school
and I saw something strange on the footage later—a lady

dressed in red in the field—and I had no explanation for it until now. And then, when I was doing the scenery for the Founder's Day show I smelled this heavy perfume in the theater and I looked up and saw a flash of red. And now I think it was *her*."

"Who?"

"May McGlynn! Oh, just come with me. See for yourselves."

The girls finish their cupcakes quickly but I can tell that they're only coming along to the exhibition to humor me.

At the exhibit with May's photograph and information they read and take it in as I back up the CD so they can hear the commentary on the headset.

"This is really interesting," Marisol says.

"It's supernatural," I correct her.

"You mean, you think you've seen a ghost and you didn't tell us?" Romy asks.

"It wasn't like I was withholding information from you. I just didn't want to believe that I was seeing something that wasn't there. I even told Mrs. Zidar in therapy. . . ."

"You saw Mrs. Zidar in therapy?" Romy is hurt.

"I made her go because of the insomnia," Suzanne explains.

"You have insomnia?" Romy is even more hurt. Why does she turn everything into something she didn't know in the first place?

"Well, you wouldn't know because you're sleeping through it."

"I'm so out of the loop." Romy sighs.

Marisol stands back, looking up at May McGlynn. "Okay, this is a sign."

"Of what?"

"Well, there's a reason that you came to the museum and found her here. She's trying to tell you something." Marisol puts her hands on her hips and squints up at May. "She's so beautiful."

"She's a movie star," I reason.

"And you make movies," Suzanne says.

"That's what Mrs. Zidar said—she said that the Red Lady was somehow related to my subconscious where art is born."

"Maybe there's a movie of hers that you're supposed to watch or something, to make some kind of connection," Suzanne says.

"There are no accidents," Marisol says definitively. "There is something here."

But what? Who is May McGlynn to me? And why did she show up in my video diaries? What does she want from me?

"Now we *have* to buy the exhibition book," Romy says. "Come on. You need her picture."

We turn to go to the gift shop. I look back at May. I swear she smiles at me, almost relieved. Or maybe I'm just imagining it.

Preparing Thanksgiving dinner at the Santrys' is about the most fun I've ever had on a holiday. There's a lot of laughter in this house, even with Mr. Santry's illness. If my dad were sick, I'd be crying all day and night, but not the Santry family. They are made of something more durable than the Chestertons for sure.

Mrs. Santry has Marisol and me peeling potatoes— sweet (for candied yams) and white (for mashed with butter). We're sitting on the screened-in porch outside the kitchen. Mrs. Santry has spread newspapers on the floor to collect the peels. I'm pretty good at peeling potatoes, but Marisol is a machine. She peels off the skin without taking any hunks out of the good stuff. Plus, she's fast.

"You okay out here?" Joe, the older Santry brother, pokes his head out of the screen door. He's also home for the holiday break. While Kevin is college cute, Joe is man cute. He has dark brown hair and blue eyes and looks a lot like Mr. Santry. He doesn't get impatient with us (not that Kevin does either), and he seems genuinely interested in where we come from and what we know.

"We're fine!" Marisol and I say in unison. Joe goes back into the kitchen.

"He is, like, ten times better-looking than Kevin," Marisol whispers.

"You know, I find it so hard not to fall in love with every older guy I see. Do you?"

"Not really. I guess I'm picky." Marisol takes the end of her potato peeler and removes a brown spot. "And I'm probably scared of them too."

"I didn't say I *wasn't* scared. I just find them so hand-some. And they're so easy to talk to." I think of Tag—who, like Joe and Kevin, is just so easy—period. "Boys our age have too many pauses in their conversations. I almost think something is wrong with them."

"This coming from a girl who has a boyfriend," Marisol teases.

"Jared is not a real boyfriend yet. I don't even know him that well." I *am* getting to know him, but I don't like to lord him over Marisol, who had a lousy time at the dance except for the conga line. I always remind myself that not everyone met a cute boy and kissed him three times at the GSA dance. I had a fluke experience, like a rainbow that comes out after a tornado in Indiana. I never brag, and I wouldn't anyway—anytime a boy likes a girl, and she likes him back, it's a delicate situation.

I look through the screen where Romy is helping Kevin make apple dumplings. She is in total bliss. Kevin seems to enjoy talking to her too but it's like talking to a little sister. I don't think Romy cares. She'll take Kevin any way she can get him.

"How's Romy doing?"

"Okay. If Kevin is Mario Batali, Romy is Rachael Ray. She's all chipper and attentive and it's like she's doing a cooking show with him," I say.

"Do you think he likes her?" Marisol asks.

"I can tell he thinks she's sweet, but he's in *college*," I remind Marisol. "This is a love that will never be."

"Not yet anyhow. She won't always be fourteen. And, they do have sports in common," Marisol says practically.

Suzanne pushes her dad into the kitchen, which has been transformed into a bakery, and up to the table. Mr. Santry places two sticks of softened butter in the bottom of a bowl, takes a couple handfuls of walnuts out of a Ziploc bag, and throws them in with the butter. Suzanne measures brown sugar into the bowl and Mr. Santry adds some cinnamon.

"Suz, warm up some cream on the stove. About three cups," Mr. Santry instructs.

After a minute, Suzanne brings the warmed cream

to the table and pours it into the bowl while Mr. Santry stirs it with his good hand. He becomes tired after a while, so Kevin takes the spoon and stirs.

Once the dough is ready, Mr. Santry helps Romy wrap an apple in a circle of dough. He shows her how to pull the dough up over the cored apple, leaving a space at the top to put the sauce.

"These are my grandmother's apple dumplings," Mr. Santry says. "I want you to learn how to make them exactly like she did."

"We're on it, Dad," Kevin assures him.

Then Romy lifts a glass dish filled with apple dumplings nestled in their pockets of dough. Mr. Santry instructs Kevin to drizzle the sauce over the top of the dumplings while Suzanne follows behind him placing small pats of butter on top of each one.

"Perfect," Mr. Santry says and smiles.

Mrs. Santry set two folding tables longways in the living room covered with a gold tablecloth with a giant paper turkey in the center, the kind with the wings that fan out. Mr. Santry is at one end of the table, and Mrs. Santry at the other. Marisol, Suzanne, and I are on one side of the table, while Romy, beaming with joy, has scored the single seat between Joe and Kevin.

"Let us bow our heads," Mr. Santry says. "We thank God for our family, our friends and our food, our good health and our good fortune. Amen."

Joe jumps up to help his dad carve the turkey, which he has a little trouble doing. Nobody says anything, but I can see that it bothers Suzanne. I pass the mashed potatoes; after all, Marisol and I killed ourselves peeling and I want everybody to try some. Kevin jokes around and Romy laughs. She's actually listened to our beauty advice and laid off the lip gloss (thank God) and is almost charming instead of annoying. In twenty-four hours, she's learned how to sit back a little and not try so hard with boys. I'm happy for her.

I lie back in the trundle in Suzanne's room, unable to sleep. I ate an entire apple dumpling by myself, and my stomach feels like a backpack loaded with rocks. I couldn't help it; the scent of butter, cinnamon, and sugar nestled on soft dough just called my name—and I responded to that call.

Suzanne sleeps on the air mattress under the windows, while Romy, who now after almost a semester at PA likes heights, sleeps in the top bunk.

Marisol, in the bottom bunk, whispers, "You awake?"

"Yeah," I tell her.

"I had too much pumpkin pie," she says. "But the filling was creamy—just enough cinnamon."

"You know, I think you ought to be a chef. You really like food."

"I know." Marisol laughs. "I like cooking more than boys. I don't know if that's a good thing."

I check my text messages. I have not heard from Jared—I sent him a turkey graphic in an email with a Happy Thanksgiving message. He did not email back and there are no text messages. Maybe he's forgotten about me. Or, maybe he has something against turkeys or national holidays in general.

"Did Jared text you?" Marisol asks.

"Not yet. Do you think he's dumped me already?"

"Hardly," Marisol says.

"You never know."

"It's the holidays. He's probably as busy as we are," Marisol whispers. "No reason to panic."

"Thanks." I'm truly grateful for sensible friends like Marisol.

"Viola, I've been thinking about the Red Lady, your May McGlynn," she says.

"Do you think I'm crazy?"

"Not at all. You never make things up. You're not hyperbolic—in fact, you're the opposite," she reasons.

"Right! I'm droll. A flatliner! And I'm not mystical at all. I don't even believe in ghosts. My friend Caitlin back in Brooklyn says I'm the least likely human being ever born to be haunted. I don't even watch scary movies. I'm not interested in other realms at all."

"I am," Marisol admits.

"You are?"

Marisol takes a deep breath. "In Mexico, there's this patron saint we revere, Our Lady of Guadalupe, and there's a shrine to her where she cries real tears. And my mother has seen it with her own eyes. She went with a group."

I sit up on my trundle bed so quickly that I have to hang on in order not to fall off of it. Marisol and Caitlin are so much alike—I just know if they ever met, they'd be BFFs. They are truly deep.

Marisol continues, "So, I *do* think it's possible that people from other realms can visit. But here's the thing. What do you do? It's not like people will understand."

"May McGlynn wants something from me, but what? Why didn't she go to the guy who directed *Slumdog Millionaire*? Why show up on my footage? I'm nobody."

"You're all she's got. She died in South Bend. She must need somebody with a camera in South Bend."

"I wish I'd never heard of May McGlynn. I'm going to

sell my camera. Then I won't have to do *anything* about this *ever*."

"Don't say that, Viola. You must never sell your camera. You're talented. Every girl in ninth grade at PA wishes she was you. You have a camera everywhere you go—it's like a purpose in life. You should be grateful for it."

Marisol makes sense. She always does. But she can afford to be supportive, because this weird stuff is not happening to *her*. And, let's face it, she's Mexican and they pray to statues and believe their icons actually weep.

And for anybody out there who thought kissing a boy three times would make everything crystal clear, as if the thing you hope for will somehow bring enlightenment and a sense of calm, forget it. It just added to my stress level. It's not *bad* stress—but it's more change, the very thing I'd like less of.

My BlackBerry flashes. I scroll down to read the message.

Jared: Happy Turkey Day—got your bird. Liked it a lot. See you soon. XO

"Who's it from?" Marisol asks. "Your boyfriend?"
"Yeah."

I text back.

Me: Safe trip back to GSA.
JS: You too.
Me: XO
JS: Double.

I sign off. Double XO's from Jared Spencer have officially made this a perfect day.

The train back to South Bend is packed with college
students from Notre Dame and Saint Mary's and Saint
Joseph's Academy. They are loud and laugh a lot, and most
of them have totes filled with Thanksgiving leftovers. We
do too. Suzanne's mom gave us each a turkey sandwich,
a bag of potato chips, and a wedge of pumpkin pie for
the ride home. Never one to save good food, I begin to
unwrap my sandwich as soon as we're on the train.

"Thanks for a great weekend," Marisol says to
Suzanne.

"I'm glad you guys could come back with me."

"Your family really made us feel at home," Romy
says.

"You mean Kevin," I say as I chew my sandwich.

"He was nice to me," Romy says without apology.

179

"Does he have a girlfriend at Marquette?"

"Yeah." Suzanne shrugs as she checks her BlackBerry. Romy is crestfallen.

Suzanne continues, "We all hate her though. She's really pretty but she's got an annoying giggle."

Romy's face is galvanized with hope.

Here is the perfect example of a sensible girl losing it the second she likes a guy. Romy knows the score. Surely she didn't think college boys just sit around without girlfriends—and study. Surely she doesn't believe that Kevin is thinking, "Romy is fourteen, but I'll wait four years until she's eighteen and then I'll ask her out." This is madness.

"Is it serious?" Romy asks Suzanne.

"Is what serious?" Suzanne puts her BlackBerry in her purse.

"Kevin and his girlfriend."

"I don't know." Suzanne shrugs again.

"Well, she didn't come home with him for Thanksgiving." Romy is persistent.

Marisol and I look at each other. I want to say to Romy, "Does it matter if it's serious? He's in *college*. He has college girls around him all day in class and all night in a coed dorm. Forget him. Find a nice guy at Grabeel Sharpe— there're a million of them and they're attainable."

"I don't think it's serious," Suzanne says in a tone that is way too encouraging. Suzanne, like all younger sisters of older brothers, is clueless about girls who like her brothers as potential boyfriends. Suzanne sees her brothers as geeks, whereas we see them as cute and older.

"Your dad seemed to have a great time," I say supportively, and as a way to change the subject.

"Yeah." Suzanne smiles. "He loves to have us all at home, and he loved having you guys there."

Jared Spencer IMs me, like, the minute we walk into Curley Kerner and drop our duffels.

JS: Are you back?
Me: Yep. Just. The picture of your baby sister is really cute.
JS: Thanks. Mom says she looks like me.
Me: Lucky her.
JS: :)
Me: Thanks for the application to the film competition. 15 to 18 minute short-subject submission? That's a lot of time to tell a story. Don't know if I can pull it off.
JS: Sure you can. You just have to choose a subject.
Me: Thinking about it. How about you?
JS: Organic farming in a shrinking farm belt.

Me: You'll win.

JS: Think so?

Me: Know so. Organic farming is so in the moment. So green. I mean, that and the melting of the polar ice cap are hot subjects.

JS: No ice cap. No funds to go and scout. Besides, the movies have to be about the Midwest. And there is only so much to say about the Midwest.

Me: Tell me about it.

JS: Gimme a sec. I have to say bye to my roomie.

I turn to the girls. "There's a film competition for high school students in the Midwest. Jared just emailed me."

"Are you going to make a movie together? How romantic!" Romy says.

"No, he's going to make a movie—maybe I'll just help him."

"Why would you do that?" Marisol wants to know.

"Why *wouldn't* I?"

"Because you film movies too. Why tag along on his? Make your own," Marisol says.

I'm about to disagree, but she's right. He sent me the application. I should think about entering a movie. I'm in high school. I'm in the Midwest. Why not?

Jared comes back online.

Me: Bus is taking us to a lecture series over at Saint Mary's College next Tuesday.

JS: Who is speaking?

Me: Wendy Luck, the performance artist. According to the flyer, she plays the flute and sings to a video narrative about her Russian/Jewish ancestry and her foremother's journey of immigration to the States.

JS: Interesting.

Me: Want to go with me?

JS: Sure.

Me: Great. I'll get the details and e you back.

JS: It's a date.

Jared signs off.

"He wants to go to the lecture series at Saint Mary's." I'm so excited to have an official date after the official first dance that my voice squeaks.

"Aren't those lectures boring?" Romy unpacks her duffel.

"Romy, it's not about the lecture. It's about Jared Spencer. It's a *date*," Suzanne says.

"It is, isn't it!" I marvel.

"Of course it is. You're going to an event, and it involves tickets and advanced planning. Therefore, it's a *date*." Suzanne says this with such authority, I can see her becoming a lawyer someday and swinging juries in her client's favor. For now, I'm sold.

I unpack my clothes and make a laundry pile to bring down to the basement. Boy, have things changed around here. I really gained some cache when I met Jared. Never underestimate cache.

It's like some miracle. I didn't see this (a real boyfriend) happening to me for years. I thought most boys were dorks (can provide a list) or unrealistic reaches (Tag Nachmanoff) or strictly pals (Andrew Bozelli) but Jared Spencer doesn't fit on any of those lists. He's cute, he's smart, and he's into the exact same things I am.

The current status of Jared and me (us) gives me a warm feeling—like I belong somewhere—even though I only have one night of talking, one full moon, and three kisses to go on. The rest I'm filling in from instant messages, pictures, and emails. I'm getting to know him, but as far as our quad is concerned, it's already a done deal—I officially have a boyfriend.

NINE

WHEN IT SNOWS IN INDIANA, IT DOESN'T FALL TO THE ground silently, melt into pools of gray slush, and then turn black from soot and traffic like it does at home in Brooklyn. Rather, it accumulates several feet deep on the ground, pristine and white, and then the wind blows it around, turning it into drifts that look like giant swirls of meringue.

As the snow blows across the flats, high winds clear paths leaving sheets of ice underneath as though somebody shoveled it, but they haven't; it's just the way it settles in South Bend.

Snow, like everything else in Indiana, is a new and different experience for me.

It's only the beginning of December, but I can already

predict that winter in the Midwest will be a doozy. It's hit freezing temperatures, so layers of snow gear—as many as I can pile on—will define the winter of 2009. Thank goodness for my mother and her anticipatory Ziploc bags full of mittens, scarves, and long underwear. My mom must've remembered the South Bend winters in the 1980s and planned ahead.

About seven girls from PA decided to take the van to Saint Mary's for lecture night. My roommates decided to sit this one out and let me brave my first real date with Jared alone. Trish is the chaperone, and her *joie* gets even worse when she's off campus and in charge of an outing. She's downright sparkly on the drive over to the college.

But so am I.

I have a date.

A real date.

My first real date.

Tickets required.

Advanced planning.

Perfect.

So far.

Jared and a few of the upperclassmen from GSA wait in the lobby of the theater. Some look at paintings displayed by Saint Mary's college students; others mill around the concession table where they sell coffee, tea, brownies, and homemade cookies. Jared waves to me as we enter the main doors. It must be forty below outside, but I don't care. I feel completely warm and welcome when I see him again. He's even cuter than he was when we met at the dance. And he seems taller as he walks toward me—not that I care so much about that.

I stomp the snow off my boots and take off my red wool hat with the giant orange pom-pom.

"Elf hat." I hold it up as Jared comes over.

"Cookie?" he asks, giving me a large chocolate chip cookie in a wax paper sleeve.

"Thanks."

I bite into the cookie, the first official food of our first official date. He preplanned the treat of the cookie, which makes me savor it even more. He had to think about what to get me before I got here, which is pretty wonderful in and of itself. If I had to imagine a perfect evening, it would be just like this—where the boy (or boyfriend!!!) actually did something nice for me without me fishing or having to ask first. Jared Spencer, you are winning my Brooklyn heart.

O'Laughlin Auditorium is a 1,300-seat theater at Saint Mary's College that is part of a larger facility called Moreau Center for the Arts. The theater is cavernous, reminding me of the big Broadway houses where my mom and dad take me to see Grand perform.

We're allowed to sit anywhere we want, so I follow Jared down the side aisle to the third row. "Is this okay?" he asks. Only about thirty of the 1,300 seats are filled.

"Sure." After we peel off our coats and gloves, we settle down into our seats to watch Wendy Luck, the flutist/singer/actor dramatize the story of her family's Russian Jewish roots.

Jared takes my hand when the lights go down, and I think between the warmth of his hand and the sweetness of the cookie, I could close my eyes and go to sleep in total bliss. But I won't. I want to be awake for every second of this date. I want to remember every detail of it, including the way his shirt has the scent of bleach, and his skin, of lemon and a little cedar. Just enough. Perfect.

I was a little worried on the way over here that Jared's feelings might have changed. What if he didn't show up? And if he did, what if he were aloof, and had decided that I wasn't the girl he remembered from the dance and that he would do what all boys seem to eventually do—second-guess his choice and drop me instantly and find somebody new who does match up to the picture in his head?

I have seen with my own eyes, time and time again, how at first a boy will act interested and then, just like the early snowflakes of December, fall in lazy, unpredictable spirals, abandon all logic, and a girl has no idea where she stands. Jared Spencer, I am finding out, is *not* one of those boys.

Miss Luck's show is good—very deep. It would do well in one of those fringe theaters in Manhattan's East Village. She is beautiful, with piercing blue eyes and a powerful singing voice. She's a good storyteller, and the story of her grandmother's trek from Minsk to Milwaukee is fascinating.

When the performance is over, Trish waves to me to meet the group at the bus stop in a few minutes. Trish honors a date when she sees one.

We go out into the lobby where Wendy Luck signs our programs. She writes: *To the cutest boy in Milwaukee* to Jared, and *I like your hat* to me.

When we leave the theater, I see Trish talking to the Saint Mary's organizer of the event. This buys me a little time alone with Jared.

He walks me toward the bus stop and threads his arm through mine. I lean on him as we walk where they've thrown down salt to melt the ice. We go carefully, not because of the ice, but because we want to slow down this night to a crawl, to squeeze in as much time as possible to be together. At least, that's what I'm hoping because that's what it feels like.

"That was a good show. Thank you for thinking of it," he says.

"Thank you for the cookie."

He smiles at me and my heart beats really fast and loud, like a banging drum in an empty theater. I'm afraid it's *too* loud, but thank God, the motor on a distant snowblower covers any strange sounds coming from me.

When we get to the bus stop, Jared reaches into his backpack. "I picked this up for you." He gives me a paperback book called *Making Movies* by Sidney Lumet. "I don't know if you have it or not."

"I don't. But I love Sidney Lumet," I tell him. "Nobody captures New York City on film better than he does." I hold the book close. My first book from Jared Spencer, and my second gift—after the cookie of course.

"It's one of the best books ever about making movies," he says.

"Thank you." When it sinks in that he actually thought of me and bought me a book about our mutual love, making movies, I blush. He'll think it's the cold temperatures but I know it's the warmth of my feelings. "How's your storyboarding going for your movie?" I ask him.

"It's going to work out. A farmer in Goshen, Indiana, who has an organic farm is letting me film there. How about you?"

When my roommates encouraged me to enter the competition, I emailed Jared right away. Not that I needed his permission, but he did tell me about the contest first, and I wanted him to know before I told anybody—including Andrew, Caitlin, and my parents—that I was entering.

"I have a sort of strange idea. I've been wondering if it would be a good subject. A plane crashed on the campus of Prefect Academy in 1925."

"Okay . . ." He listens.

"Onboard was a young actress destined to be a great movie star, like Bette Davis or Joan Crawford or Myrna Loy. But the plane crashed and she died before she fulfilled her potential and became a big star."

"What's the story?"

"*That's* the story. Her story."

"No, no . . ." Jared smiles. "I mean, what's your take on the story?"

"I guess I'm not sure yet." The snow crunches under my feet as I shift by the bus stop.

"You don't have to have all the answers just yet," Jared says. "But tell me more about the actress."

"Okay, well, when I went home with Suzanne for Thanksgiving, her mom took us to the the Art Institute of Chicago. And they had an exhibit about Midwestern Americans and their contribution to American movies. And I was walking through and read about the actress who died in the crash. Her name was May McGlynn. And it's sort of ironic that she died on the PA campus since I'm going to school there." I conveniently leave out the part about how I think she's been haunting me. This is only our second date after all.

"It's the start of something." Jared buries his hands in his pockets. "You know, it's all about the story. What are you trying to say? And why tell it? You have to answer those questions before you begin to break down the story into scenes and write the script."

I lift up the Sidney Lumet book. "Are the answers in here?"

He laughs. "A few of them."

"Well, guess what I'm going to stay up and read tonight?"

Jared looks at storytelling in a way that I don't. I learned how to make movies from my parents, who have worked in documentary nonfiction. Generally they do not plan ahead; they immerse themselves in a world and find the story after filming hours of footage. It's a definite style—to film everything you can about a subject and then get into editing and find the through-line. Jared has an entirely different approach. You choose a subject, develop a story, and *then* you pick up your camera.

The bus from GSA pulls up first in front of the bus stop. My heart sinks. I don't want this night to end. Nothing is as good as being together and actually having real conversations. Texting is okay, and emailing is fine, but I just like being with Jared—the two of us. Talking. I wonder if he feels the same.

Jared turns to board. "You know, I wish we had more time," he says, almost reading my thoughts.

"I know. Me too." I look off into the snow drifts, and everything seems impossible—like spring will never come and Jared and I will never have enough time to hang out and get to know each other.

"Well, this will have to do," he says. Then he leans down and kisses me. This time I'm able to appreciate the kiss because I was more prepared, and anticipated it. I keep my eyes closed just a few seconds longer; then we say good-bye.

I open my eyes.

My fourth kiss, this one at the bus stop on the Saint Mary's College campus in South Bend, Indiana, right after a blizzard. I'm counting this kiss, adding it to the three previous kisses. Of course I'm counting! Four kisses, one hand-holding, one giant chocolate chip cookie, and one Sidney Lumet book. I think I have an actual boyfriend. Jared waves to me from the window as the bus pulls away from the stop.

The van from PA pulls up in front of the bus stop. I climb in, holding my book.

"Whatcha got there?" Trish asks as she bounds up the steps behind me.

"Sidney Lumet's book about making movies."

"Coo," she says.

I have a few goals for my time at the Prefect Academy, and one of them is to get my RA to put an *L* at the end of *cool* when she uses the word. "Yeah. Very," I tell her. But I'm in a forgiving mood. "It's very, very coo." I laugh.

When I get back to the quad, Suzanne is reading in her bunk while Romy works at her desk. Marisol is at the library.

Suzanne looks up excitedly. "How did it go?"

"Great," I admit. "He gave me a book."

"A present on the first official date? This is major," Romy exclaims.

"I know. I wasn't sure he'd actually show up, and he did."

"You have to have some confidence. Jared Spencer is crazy about you. Trust me. I know," Suzanne promises.

"Did he kiss you again?" Romy asks.

I nod. "A good-bye kiss in the snow."

"God, this is so romantic. Kissing in the snow. I mean, it's a movie, even if you guys weren't movie geeks—your love affair is so cinematic," Marisol says.

"I wouldn't call it a love affair."

"I would!" Romy says. And she would—believe me, if she got Kevin Santry to kiss her, it would be on the main page of the PA newsblog. She'd probably do a blast to the entire freshman class announcing the liplock.

"I really like him," I tell the girls. "He bought me a cookie and he let me choose our seats for the show."

"How suave." Romy lies down on her bed with a dreamy look on her face—no doubt thinking of Kevin Santry.

I undress and get into my pajamas, pulling on my robe for extra warmth. I jiggle the radiator steam release to throw some more heat into our room.

I look out the alcove windows. The fountain, covered in snow, looks like the whipped cream on top of a sundae. The sculpture of fish is covered in a drift, and the snow is so deep, you can't see the bench. Even our windowsills are covered in white up to the sash.

I grab my laptop and climb into bed, pulling the covers up. I instant message Andrew.

Me: You there?

AB: How's it going?

Me: I went to a lecture tonight with Jared.

AB: I went to Olivia's to study.

Me: How's it going?

AB: Great.

Me: That's nice. I'm coming home for Christmas. I hope you can carve out some time for me.

AB: Of course. R U crazy?

Me: What about Olivia?

AB: What about her?

Me: Will she mind?

AB: I'll send her to the beauty parlor when you're home. That will take 6 days.

Me: Uh-oh.

AB: What?

Me: Trouble in the love zone?

AB: Nah.

Me: Glad to hear it.

AB: What about Jared?

Me: He's going home to Milwaukee.

AB: Sure, we can hang.

Me: Great. I have lots to tell you.

AB: Cool.

Me: I mean a lot. About everything.

AB: I get it.

Me: Great.

Something very strange is happening with my BFFAA. Andrew and I used to talk once a day, and now we talk once a week. He doesn't really want to video conference and sometimes when I IM him, he doesn't respond right away, whereas when I lived at home, it was like he was sitting there waiting to hear from me. We've always had instant access to each other. But it's almost as though the moment he got a girlfriend, I got bumped. I never thought that would ever happen! Even looking to the future, if we go to colleges in different states, I figured we'd stay solid. I thought Andrew and I were a for-sure, forever-and-always team. Dating (his and mine) has done strange things to my old friend.

Sometimes I wonder if Suzanne is right—maybe Andrew is jealous of Jared. But that's just too weird. We know each other so well.

When I go home to New York for break, one of the

first things I will do, after ordering in doubles of cold noodles with sesame sauce from Sung Chu Mei, will be to walk across the Brooklyn Bridge into Manhattan to go to Scoop in the Village. After I've bought myself one nice thing, I will sit down with Andrew face-to-face and say, "What the eff? What happened to us? Let's remember who we are and what we came from." I'm going to say it just like that. And I can't wait to hear what he says.

The Christmas season was practically invented for people like Trish. She's the kind of person who has twinkling white lights in her ficus tree year-round and, as soon as Thanksgiving passes, puts a wreath crammed with glass balls on her door and displays her collection of vintage elves on her nightstand. She is *so* into it. Surprise.

The seniors are in charge of gathering and creating evergreen garlands for each floor. They have a hot chocolate party and go into the woods with hacksaws to pick the best greens.

The juniors make the red velvet bows to go on the garlands, which is an easy job because from the looks of it, they just save the bows year to year and pass them down. Basically, they unpack boxes as their contribution to holiday cheer.

The sophomores decorate the tree in the entrance hall,

which is ginormous and has old-fashioned Roma lights in red, green, and blue threaded through the branches. There is an ornate brass menorah in the window, and just to make sure all bases are covered, Kwanzaa candles are lit in the dining hall.

The freshmen are basically the grunts for the sophomores, and we also have to sign up for caroling groups to go into South Bend and sing for the locals.

To top it all off, the school gardener places nondenominational sprays of evergreens on the entrance doors to the main buildings. The atriums have a million pots of poinsettias and webs of twinkling white lights on the ceilings, which are pretty at night. Ho. Ho. Ho.

I go online about seventy times a day to check the status of my flight home on December twentieth with a return on January third. I'm flying out of O'Hare in Chicago. I'm worried about blizzards, malfunctioning engines, and the fine-print problem where the airlines give up your seat without alerting you. If that happens to me, I will pitch a hissy fit. Nothing can prevent me from going home! If I have to go by dogsled, I will be in Brooklyn for Christmas.

Trish is going to drive me to the airport and even two hours of torture stuck in a car, just her and me, cannot for one second quell my excitement at getting home, back to my neighborhood, my room, and my world.

"Everybody is totally jealous of you and Jared," Marisol says as we drape the garland down the center of our hall.

"Marisol, getting a boyfriend is not an achievement in life." I climb the ladder to secure the garland to the ceiling.

"You can say that because you have one," Marisol says, spotting me from the floor.

"I guess that's true." I make a loop with the garland through a hook.

"You were the least likely in our quad to find personal happiness."

I climb down the ladder. "Why do you say that?"

"You didn't throw yourself into the PA experience."

"For the record, I don't throw myself into much. Except film."

"I know." We're quiet for a few minutes, unwinding more garland. Marisol is unusually quiet. I feel bad. I know I talk about Jared a lot. Marisol doesn't seem to mind, but still.

"What's up with you? You don't seem like yourself." I watch her face and she just shrugs, looking even sadder.

"I just found out I can't go home for Christmas break."

"What?" Now I feel horrible that I've been talking

nonstop about breaking out of here for the holidays.

"Mom and Dad are going down to Mexico to be with my grandmother. They think this could be her last Christmas."

"And they're going to leave you here?" I'm shocked.

"They can't afford to bring me home and go take care of my grandmother. So I volunteered to stay here because I knew it would be easier for them."

The idea of Marisol getting stuck at the Prefect Academy over Christmas vacation practically breaks my heart. "I know! Maybe my folks could drive out and you can come home with me."

"Do you think?" A smile begins to creep across her face.

"My parents are totally flexible. They'd love it."

"My parents would be so happy that I wasn't alone on Christmas."

"Consider it done!"

As Marisol and I hang the garland, I tell her everything about New York. She's never been there, and boy, is she in for the trip of a lifetime. Wait until she sees the Empire State Building and the Hudson River and the Saks Christmas windows. I'll take her to see *The Nutcracker* at the New York City Ballet! She won't have time to miss her parents. It will be a whirlwind of fun.

The work tables in Hojo's film classroom are long and deep. Suzanne, Romy, and Marisol sit across from me as I lay out my plans to make a movie about May McGlynn.

"I'd like to thank you all for taking time out of your busy skeds to meet me here."

"Knock it off, Viola. It's just us." Suzanne opens her notebook.

"Sorry."

"We could have met in our room," Romy complains. "We have snacks."

"No, I want this to be . . . professional," I tell them. I give each of the girls a printout of my proposal for the movie that I want to make and submit to the Midwest Secondary School Film Competition. Ever since talking with Jared about it, I've been thinking and thinking.

As the girls read, I tap my pencil nervously on the work table. I look out on the grounds, where a group of sophomores return from snowshoeing in the great woods behind our school.

"Okay." Suzanne puts down the paper.

"I'm done," Marisol says.

"Me too." Romy looks at me.

"What do you guys think?"

"This is a life story that has it all. May is a young and beautiful starlet," Marisol says. "Then fate steps in."

"She dies young," I say. "Okay, here's what I'm thinking. She tells her life story at the site of the crash."

"Cool. I like it," Romy says.

"I'm directing and shooting the film with my camera. I need a producer to do the budget. I need a costume and set designer and I need actors. This is where you guys come in. . . ."

"I don't know how I can help. I'm not arty at *all*," Romy says.

"You don't have to be. A producer handles the budget. And you're really good with math." I give Romy an envelope. "My mom forwarded me a sample budget for a short-subject film, and I thought you could create one for me. I'm going to film on video and cut it on my own Avid, but part of the competition is that you have to show a budget."

"Okay. I'll figure it out." Romy opens the envelope and unfolds the document.

"And Marisol, you have a good eye. I thought you could do costume and scenery. Mrs. Hawfield in the costume shop said that you could pull whatever you needed. Here's the permission slip."

"Sounds like fun."

"So what do I do? Make the popcorn for the pre-miere?" Suzanne laughs.

"No, you're going to play May McGlynn."

"The dead girl? Cool!" Suzanne high-fives Romy. "I never thought I'd be in a movie!"

"Principle photography will commence February first, here on campus. The deadline for submission to the contest is March tenth, so I figure we'll film for three days, and then I'll do my edit and submit by the deadline."

"We're really going to make a movie? Really? Quad 11 is actually going into show business!" Romy is enthralled. Her blue streaks have practically disappeared from her red hair, and she's let her bob grow out. I think she's going for a more sophisticated look, probably to appear older to Kevin Santry whenever they meet again.

"I'll have a script to you guys by Christmas break, so you can prepare."

I feel very *Hollywood* promising everyone on my team a script. But like every writer who ever had an idea, I only have the germ of it. I have the character of May—and a life story that ended in tragedy. Is that enough? I hope I will find the story as I'm writing. I'll be calling on my muses to guide me—including May McGlynn.

TEN

FINAL EXAMS FOR THE FIRST SEMESTER ARE ALMOST over. Grabeel Sharpe delivered toys to needy kids, and I agreed to go with Jared, but at the last minute, with the possibility of failing the ninth-grade bio exam, I decided to stay in and try to pass the thing. We haven't had another date. So, as of December 9, 2009, I'm in a holding pattern of four kisses, one hand-holding, one date, one cookie, and one book. The IMs and texts are at, like, a record-breaking number at this point. When you add it all up, it's perfectly great (because I wasn't expecting anything at all in the social department), but I've also learned, with the guidance of Suzanne, to never count on much when it comes to boys, because then you will not be disappointed. So far, that's become the backbone of my romantic philosophy. My good luck and excellent fortune with Jared

Spencer has lasted longer than Trish's box of salt water taffy that she opens when you go into her room to discuss "problems." This, in my life, is a triumph already.

While I'm studying for the bio exam, an email pops up from my mom to turn on the video conference camera. I push my hair behind my ears and sit up, waving to my mom through the computer.

"Hi, Mom!"

"Viola, you look tired."

"It's final exams. I *am* tired."

"Are you drinking your fizzy Emergen-C powder every day?" she asks.

"Yep."

"Good. That will ward off colds."

My dad nestles into the shot next to my mother.

"Hey, kid," he says.

"Dad, you have to shave that beard before I come home. Your face looks like Davy Crockett's hat."

"Don't you like it?"

"No. I want my old dad back."

"Sorry." He smiles.

My dad usually grows a beard when he's filming. My mother also lets her personal appearance go when she's working. I see a half inch of gray roots on top of the brown with the caramel highlights from early fall.

"So, how are you?" Mom says.

"Well, I think you will be happy to know that I've decided to embrace this place for another semester. I'm going to stop bugging you to quit your movie."

"What changed your mind?" Dad wants to know as he takes Mom's hand in victory (for now) and solidarity.

"I'm making a movie."

"I got your proposal. It's terrific," Dad says. "I'm happy you decided to enter the competition."

"Thanks. I think it will be an amazing experience to make my first film here. There's something to be said for creating works of art in a quiet vacuum. . . ."

"Now, Viola . . ." Mom begins to correct my lousy attitude.

"Just kidding. I'm getting into it. I have it *slightly* cast—my roommate Suzanne is playing the lead—and I'll write the script when I'm home."

"We want to talk to you about that," Mom says, making a face that sends a web of small lines across her forehead.

"What's the matter?"

"Honey, we can't get to the States for Christmas."

"What are you talking about? Marisol is coming with me—didn't you get my email about driving out to get us?"

"And we would have, except that now we can't be there."

"I can't believe you're putting your stupid project before me," I say, furious.

"It's not like that at all. This is very painful for us. And we talked to Mrs. Grundman, the headmistress—"

"You told *her* before me?"

"We had to make arrangements with her," Dad interjects.

"This is just great. You go behind my back and make plans without asking me first?" Tears sting my eyes.

"It's not as bad as it sounds. We actually have good news in all of this." My mother looks at my father and then into the camera to me. "Grand is going to go to South Bend and spend Christmas with you."

"That's supposed to make up for you not being here?"

"Now, Viola, you love Grand. You'll have a ball with her." Dad's tone is stern.

"She's starting rehearsals for a Broadway play after the first of the year, and this will be her last vacation for a long time," Mom says. "She's dying to see you, honey. And Mrs. Grundman assures me that they have a wonderful Christmas dinner planned, and one of the guest rooms in Curley Kerner is reserved for Grand."

"You planned all of this without once thinking to ask me."

"We knew how disappointed you'd be and we wanted to make sure you could have the best Christmas possible if we couldn't be there with you."

I think about home. I think about my BFFAA Andrew and how our friendship is basically in tatters, shredded to the point where I may have to drop the AA and go to plain BFF. I think about my room, and the East River at night, and the Christmas moon over Brooklyn and how it feels like I'm never going to see any of what matters to me ever again. I'm a refugee from normal family life. I have no place to go. I'm more marooned now than I was when I landed here in September.

"Viola?" Dad says gently.

I wait before answering him. Then I wipe my eyes on my sleeve. "What?"

"I know you can't understand this now, and that this is really difficult for you, but in the realm of choices we had regarding Christmas, we chose the best one for you."

"Yeah, right."

"Our hearts are broken that we can't be with you." My mother begins to cry. "You're our world."

Well, that's not exactly true, is it, Mom? But I don't say that out loud. If I was *your world*, as you say, wouldn't you leave the one you're in to be with me?

Jared Spencer puts his arm around me outside Curley Kerner. The maintenance man, Mr. Jackowski, clears the benches of snow. Maybe because some of the faculty of PA are so decrepitly old that he's afraid they might keel over in the drifts, freeze to death, and not be found until Easter break, if they don't have a place to stop and rest.

We wander for a while across the campus. Jared got a ride over to PA with an upperclassman who was meeting one of our senior girls so we could see each other before Christmas. Jared Spencer is a good advance planner—it makes me like him more, and of course, makes him an organized filmmaker. Jared's dad is picking him up at GSA tonight, and Jared will go home for the two-week break.

"What do you think you'll do for the break?" Jared asks.

"Marisol will be here, so I guess we'll hang out. And my grandmother is coming. And I have to write the script for my movie."

"I'm going to write my script over break too," he says. "Though I've already done most of the work."

"You're kidding. When did you find the time?"

"I like writing more than just about anything, so I do

it before school work. It won't be a good scene when my grades arrive."

We stand by the trees in front of the Geier-Kirshenbaum classroom building and look at each other. The wind carries a clump of snow from the trees that falls on my face, stinging me. Jared quickly wipes the snow off with his gloved hands and then looks at me for a long while. Of all the things I like most about having a boyfriend, and believe me, the list is pretty long, the best is when we're alone—and we don't say anything—we just look at each other. Suzanne says every person ever born likes to be adored, and I guess I fit very comfortably into that group.

"Are you ready to exchange gifts?" Jared asks.

"Absolutely."

Jared and I planned to see each other before Christmas. It's not been easy, with finals and all the school activities centered around the holidays, but we have managed to get together because he made it happen.

We each pull packages out of our backpacks.

"You first," he says to me. I open a slim, square package. It's a black-and-white clapperboard and comes with its own box of chalk. The gift is so perfect and so personal and so supportive of my dreams that I don't have to fake how thrilled I am. Jared Spencer thinks of everything.

"I love it. Thank you!" I throw my arms around him and give him a hug.

Then he opens his package from me.

"This is great. I really need this," he says, looking down at the updated two-disc set computer program for the Avid. "I can't wait to try it."

"It's all the bells and whistles. You can even do subtitles and crawlers with it."

"Really?"

"Yeah. I can show you how. After Christmas."

"Cool," he says.

"Hey, Jared?" Jared's ride, a GSA senior named Paul, waves from the parking lot. "Gotta go, brother," he says.

"I gotta go," Jared says.

"I heard," I say and smile.

"Sorry." And then Jared Spencer leans down and kisses me softly, gently—perfectly. "Merry Christmas," he says. "It'll go fast."

"Merry Christmas."

One dance, one lecture, one outside walking date, five kisses, one cookie, one book, and one most excellent clapperboard for movie production. I watch Jared go as the wind blows more snow onto me. But this time, the snow doesn't sting my face, my tears do. And I'm not crying for Jared Spencer—okay, partly, I really like him a lot—I'm crying because Christmas, and my hopes for a perfect one, keep leaving me.

As I walk back to Curley Kerner, I think about all the positive things that have happened to me since I came to the Prefect Academy. I've made good friends and I've had challenging classes and I'm planning my first movie. I met Jared. There are many good things to be grateful for, so why do I feel abandoned? My parents sent me to PA for the *education* and the *experience*, and I could accept that, if only I were able to go home for Christmas. I wonder if I'll ever find my way back home. Brooklyn seems like a million miles away.

"Where's my girl?" I hear Grand's voice thunder in the entrance hall of Curley Kerner. My grandmother's loud, deep, and clear voice is truly her signature as an actress and as a human being. It's the kind of voice that can clear a gymnasium full of people with one well-timed holler of: *"Fire!"*

"I'm on my way!" I call down the stairs. I'm happy that she's here—three days with only Marisol and six other students with no place to go for the holidays has been boring. I've been working on my movie script, and when I'm not writing, I join the girls for down time. We watch DVDs, hang out, and go to the University Park

Mall with Mrs. Zidar in the school van . . . to shop. For whom? I always wonder as we board the van. But I ended up getting Grand a pair of Isotoner gloves (she'll need them around here in the bitter cold) and a chic thermos for her dressing room when she's in a play.

Grand stands in the center of the entrance hall with her hands on her hips. She wears a black cossack hat and a white down coat with small, puffy stitched windows that reaches to her ankles. "There you are!" She beams at me, wide and full just like my mother, who has the same smile.

I skip down the steps and into her arms. "Thank God you're here."

"I wouldn't want to be anywhere else!" she says.

As she hugs me for a long time, I let her. I really need a good hug from someone I'm related to. Grand smells like oranges and cream, and her skin is soft. She's always bugging my mom to take care of her skin too, but Mom just doesn't have the time to follow through with a beauty regimen.

The doors of the entrance hall swing open. A tall, very handsome man carrying a bunch of suitcases pushes through and puts the bags on the floor.

"I want you to meet George," Grand says, well, grandly.

"Hi, George."

"Hello, Viola. I've heard a lot about you." He has one of those very white, very bright smiles that you see in the after pictures in dental ads.

"I've never heard a word about you, George," I tell him honestly.

He and Grand burst out laughing. "I told you she was funny," Grand says to him.

"George and I are friends," Grand says, dropping her voice about two octaves when she says the word *friends*, like it's a secret or something.

"I'm nuts about your grandmother," he says.

"Doesn't he look like Cary Grant?" she says. "You know, sophisticated and uptown?"

"Viola won't know who he is," George says.

"The heck! I taught her everything there was to know about screwball comedies, right, Viola?"

"Yep. My favorite is Cary Grant and Irene Dunne in *The Awful Truth*, and you do look like him."

"Yeah, well, I'd like his film career," George says without sounding one bit jealous.

My grandmother (the good news) showed up for Christmas break, but she brought her boyfriend (what?). And this man is, like, my mom's age, somewhere in his forties, I'm guessing, because he has gray hair at the temples—or maybe he's in his fifties and gets facials, I don't know—but any way around it, he's a lot younger than my grandmother, who happens to be sixty-four years old exactly. But she doesn't look sixty-four. She has long blond hair and a trim figure, and she wears very good pancake makeup with a bronze blush that makes her look robust. Grand is described as willowy in theatrical reviews—from her ingenue days until now.

"Go ahead, Viola. Tell George what you know about screwball comedies." Grand removes her cossack hat and shakes her head. Her blond hair tumbles out onto her shoulders.

"Right, right. Sorry. I like to focus on films made in Hollywood from 1933 to 1943," I tell him.

"Which ones?" Grand steps back and gives me the floor to speak.

"Well . . . I like movies about runaway heiresses. Three of my favorites are *It Happened One Night*, *Midnight*, and *My Man Godfrey*, which had particular social significance because it was released during the Great Depression and dealt with themes of homelessness in the form of the 'forgotten men' as portrayed by William Powell. Now, if we're talking Cary Grant, there's the aforementioned *The Awful Truth* and *Bringing Up Baby* where he uses physical comedy to express his inner emotional turmoil. And you do resemble him, George, but I think you look a little more like Rock Hudson in *Pillow Talk*."

"There's nothing to sneeze at in terms of comedy with that one," Grand interjects.

"It was very good," I tell them. "But *Pillow Talk* came out in 1959, so it doesn't exactly fit my screwball list. So, are you an actor?"

"Just a working stiff, Viola." George smiles at me. It's hard not to like him.

"Darling . . . ," Grand says. She turns to me. "He's modest! George is a *brilliant* actor. He's the lead in the revival of *Arsenic and Old Lace*."

"Who do you play?" I ask Grand.

"Aunt Abby. With a lot of age makeup." She makes a face. "We start rehearsals after New Year's at the Cincinnati Playhouse in the Park. The very same theater where I triumphed as Ophelia," Grand explains.

"How did you guys meet?" I ask.

"At auditions." George puts his arm around Grand.

"I always pooh-poohed the idea of soul mates, but when I met George, I believed at long last in the concept of it. Two people . . ." Grand waves her hand through the air like she's unfurling one of those Japanese twirling ribbons. "Two lives yet one perspective, one world view. Am I right, George?"

I don't want to interrupt Grand as she defines her love for George, and I remind her that she said the exact same thing about her last two boyfriends, one of whom was a director and the other a venerable lighting designer. Evidently, you can have a lot of soul mates in one lifetime. Grand unpeels them out of the pack like Life Savers out of the foil wrapper.

"You're right, doll," George says and smiles. I find it so funny that he's calling Grand a *doll*, when she's the one who looks like she's playing with one. That wasn't very nice of me—to even think such a thing—but this Christmas is so deeply and profoundly ruined anyhow that being Princess Snark isn't going to make it any worse.

"Would you like to see your room?" I ask.

"We spoke with Mrs. Headmistress . . ."

"Mrs. Grundman?"

"Right. Right. That's the name! And she made sure we have *two* rooms reserved." Grand looks at George with the "I'm setting a good example for my granddaughter" look.

"Great. Whatever." I shrug. I figure when you're sixty-four you can do whatever you want, but if Grand wants to set a good example, why not let her? They're going to be performing their own screwball comedy running from her room to his or whatever in the cold hallway of the guest wing, but that's none of my business.

George picks up the suitcases. I help with a small carry-on and show them down to the basement, past the laundry room, beyond the rec room, where the guest rooms are located at the end of a long hallway.

As Grand and George follow me down the stairs, they laugh and joke like a very happy couple. I notice, for the record, that Jared and I are way more low-key and digni-fied. Grand and George are almost silly.

"Here they are." I point to the entrances to the fur-nished guest rooms. "No smoking in the building," I remind them.

"Oh, I haven't smoked since the sixties." Grand laughs.

"And I wasn't born yet," George jokes.

"Oh, you!" she says and laughs again.

This is going to be one bizarre Christmas, I think as I climb the stairs back up to our quad.

ELEVEN

"NOW, GIRLS. EVEN THOUGH WE'RE HERE IN . . ."
Grand has to think. A true actress, she has to think what
town she is in when she lands, because she travels to
a different city every night when she's on tour. "South
Bend, we want to make this Christmas as homespun as
possible, don't we?" Grand says as she sits on the edge
of my bed.

There is not one *thing* homespun about my grandmother, and to put her in charge of anything cozy spells
disaster. She is not a woman who keeps antique dolls on
her bed or has anything crocheted in her apartment—
except for a bikini from the seventies.

Grand's home is an ultra-modern apartment on the
Upper East Side of Manhattan, a rent-controlled (this

means that my mom doesn't worry about my grandmother ever losing the apartment and its low rental fee),
sunny one bedroom with a terrace. She has wild plants
and a Buddha shrine on the terrace (the only Buddha
on the terrace of an Upper East Side apartment, she
believes). She has simple tangerine leather furniture and
giant paintings of single peaches and a giant artichoke.
She's not an arts-and-crafts grandmother with a ceramic
beehive cookie jar at *all*. I don't know if I can trust her
with our Indiana Christmas.

"I suppose we'll need a tree," she says.

"That's homey," Marisol agrees. Of course, she sleeps
under a quilt patched together with uneven stitches and
actual handwriting on it, so she's totally into rustic.

"We should celebrate the holiday with a tip of the hat
to our various ethnic backgrounds," Grand says. "Now,
I'm of English and Irish descent—as is Viola."

"I thought Cerise was French," Marisol says.

"Coral Cerise is Grand's stage name. Her real-life
name is Carol Butler."

"Oh." Marisol looks at me, confused. I'm so used to my
theatrical grandmother (my dad calls her The Mother-
In-Law of Reinvention behind her back) that it didn't
even dawn on me to tell Marisol that Grand changed her
name, or even how many times Grand changed it.

Originally, my grandmother was born Carol Evelyn Gray. She married my grandfather and she became Carol Gray Butler. Then after she divorced him, she overhauled everything, her home, her wardrobe, and her name, changing the Carol to Coral ("I never felt like a Carol," she explained), and became Coral Gray. And then finally Coral Cerise when she went to a psychic who said that Grand's greatest success in the American theater would come after the age of fifty and *only* if she changed her name. When she changed her name to Cerise, everyone thought she was remarried (which she wasn't). My mom said that the psychic probably said Charisse, after the great dancer Cyd Charisse but Grand misheard and wrote down Cerise. Anyhow, now, and for the immediate future, she will probably remain Coral Cerise.

"In New York we read a play aloud at Christmas." Grand goes to our alcove and looks out over the grounds. "It's a family tradition, so let's do that here as well."

"Last year we read *A Christmas Carol*," I tell Marisol. "Another year we read *George Washington Crossing the Delaware* and *Bertha, Queen of Norway* by Kenneth Koch."

"Guess who played the queen?" Grand smiles.

"That sounds like fun. And with you and George being professional actors, I bet it will be something." Marisol easily gets on the theatrical Christmas bus.

"What are your family traditions, Marisol?"

"Well, we collect brown paper bags all fall and then we line them up on the walkway to our house and put votive candles in them and light them on Christmas Eve."

Grand makes a sort of horrified face and then says, "Lovely."

"Oh, and we go to Mass," Marisol says. She gets in the van with the Catholics every Sunday morning and they head over to Saint Mary's College for church. Marisol said at the beginning of the semester, there were, like, twenty girls and by Christmas break, about three who go, not including the old ladies from Saint Joe's rest home who they pick up along the way.

"We'll all go to Mass with you," Grand says.

"That would be nice."

"George will drive. He's Polish and must be Catholic— isn't that country ninety percent Catholic? And I've asked Mrs. Grundman if we can make our own dinner in the kitchen, and she agreed."

"Whew. We dodged a bullet with that one. The only turkey we have on campus is pressed."

"We'll get a real bird, then." Grand makes a list. "Now, is there anything else you girls would like?"

Marisol gets tears in her eyes. "Can you take us home?"

"Now, Marisol, there will be none of that. NO tears. I'm an actress, and I'm the only one allowed to have a good sob because I actually get paid to let 'em flow like old Niagara Falls. I promise you will look back on this Christmas when you're my age . . . fifty-two-ish, and you will say, that was a great Christmas. Offbeat, original, and totally different. Trust me. I know how to do holidays."

Marisol wipes her eyes. "Okay, Miss Cerise."

There are a few nuns, a couple of maintenance people, and Grand, Marisol, George, and me at Christmas-morning Mass at the Chapel of Our Lady of Loretto on the Saint Mary's College campus. I hope the priest doesn't die during the service. He's so old that he actually might. But at least George is in good shape and he's big enough to carry the man out in a worst-case scenario.

The chapel is very pretty with a high ceiling and lots of tiny tiles on the walls in shades of blue. The chocolate brown wooden benches and matching altar make for a very nice color scheme.

It ends up that George Dvorksy is in fact a Catholic. And evidently, as a bonus, he was an altar boy, so he can help Father Time (literally) say the Mass. George has to put items on the altar and ring bells. Every once in a while George looks up from his sacred duties and winks at Grand. Holy. Holy. Holy.

I can see that Marisol is comforted by her rituals, and I think of my own: how my parents would come to get me on Christmas morning, and we'd go up the stairs where the tree was lit and Christmas presents were everywhere. Mom and Dad would cook, and have their friends over—people who had kids my age—like Lily Kamp with her parents; the Rosenfelds with Anna, Kate, and Jane; the Dyjas with Nick and Kay; and the Prietos with Emilio and Aaron. Mary Ehlinger often came over and read aloud from the poetry of Edgar Guest. And pets were allowed, so there were a couple of dogs—Elvis and Click. We'd all play together while our parents would sit around and talk and laugh.

The talking and the laughing is the music that I miss the most—that, and my parents calling my name to "gather the troops" for dinner. Grand would always show up later, because she sleeps in (all actresses do—never call one before noon or they shoot to kill), and she'd bring one of her boyfriends. So, on that level, the Grand level, it isn't so odd—George Dvorsky would have fit in at the brownstone—and Mom and her friends would have drunk wine in the kitchen and gone on and on with deep admiration about how young George is, and how amazing a person Grand is to attract such peppy dates.

When it comes time to read from what looks from

back here like the Bible, the old priest motions to my grandmother who puts her hand on her chest and mouths *Me?* I whisper, "Yes, you," because Father Time doesn't mean any of the nuns, who seem to have their heads bowed in prayer but are actually asleep.

Grand gets up and out of the pew and sashays to the podium. She pulls her chic reading glasses out of the pocket of her slim wool skirt and reads, "It came to pass in those days that there went out a decree from Caesar Augustus . . ." And then Grand does the weirdest thing: She starts crying. And George gets up from his little bench next to Father Time and joins her. He reads aloud where she has left off, and when she pulls herself together, she takes over and tells the rest of the story—which everyone knows—about the poor girl, fifteen and pregnant, and her husband, Joseph, and full-up hotels unable to take them.

Father Time has us all sing "Joy to the World" a capella when the service is over, and Marisol and I belt it out really loud to make up for the deaf nuns. Grand and George hold hands as we go. I'm amazed that I had a spiritual experience, and I wasn't even looking for it.

Marisol and I clear the dishes from the dining-hall table. Grand made turkey and stuffing and yams and green bean casserole. We invited the league of nations girls: the two Africans, three Central Europeans, and one Canadian who couldn't go home for the holidays. Grand and George acted out small scenes from *Arsenic and Old Lace*, which were very funny and doubled as practice for when they return "to the boards" after Christmas. Now everyone else has gone back to Curley Kerner to watch movies, while we sit with Grand and George.

"I'm good at dishes," George says. "Marisol, want to help me out?"

"Sure!" she says.

"We'll be in to help shortly," Grand calls after him. She turns to me and asks, "Did you talk to your parents today?"

"We video conferenced. Mom cried through the whole thing."

"She doesn't have my stiff upper lip," Grand laments. "Never did. Thank God she didn't go into the theater."

"I thought it was nice that she missed me. But she should have thought of that before she decided not to come home. My parents are the most selfish people on the planet."

"Viola . . . ," Grand says in a warning tone.

"It's true. They dumped me here."

"Dumped you? Young lady, you are out of line." Grand

is not using her actress voice. It's real. She's angry with me. "You're accusing your mother of deliberately missing an opportunity to be with you, and that's just not true."

"I'm an only child. There are girls here with, like, ten siblings and somehow their parents manage to get here and bring them home for Christmas. My parents passed. They couldn't even get it together to carve out, like, three days to see me."

"Viola, there's a good reason for that."

"Well, I'd like to hear it." I know my parents well. They're artists. They become so absorbed in their work they don't hear things like the phone, the doorbell, or the smoke alarm. All my life, I've been the one to snap them out of their creative comas. Grand knows this. And I don't care if it sounds sarcastic, I think it's wrong for parents to abandon their children on holidays. It scars them for life—whether the parents have a good reason or not. At least Marisol's parents blew her off for a life-and-death cause. For my parents, it's just work. "They care about their projects more than me."

"That's not true. Your parents can't afford to come home financially."

My mind reels. In all my life, my parents never acted like we *didn't* have money. There didn't seem to be a lot, but there didn't appear to be too little, either. Yes, they are frugal, but that's because they use all their money to finance their movies. They rent out a floor of the brownstone fixer-upper to a professor from Pratt, and sometimes they take jobs they don't want their names on (like a certain hour-long TV drama that shot in New York City and was canceled after, like, two episodes). I know we're not rich; we don't go on vacations (that's usually because they travel so much—it's almost dumb to go on vacation somewhere besides our home to rest), but money never seems to be an issue. The filmmakers and artists my parents know aren't rich either, but I never, ever thought of them as poor. "Grand, what are you talking about?"

"I'm talking about a bad run of financial reversals and no jobs."

"Dad and Mom were developing their own projects."

"When the paying gigs dried up."

"Why didn't they tell me?"

"They didn't want you to worry. And Viola, I didn't tell you this to have you worry. You're smart and you're mature and you can handle knowing the truth. I told you so that you might see things through their eyes."

"They could have cut corners by keeping me at home— this place is expensive!"

"I'm paying for it," Grand says.

The reality of *that* hits me like a rock in the face. Grand should not be spending her hard-earned money on me—that's crazy! She's one year from retirement age. (Though, if you were to use her version of the math, she's got an additional thirteen years.)

"And I'm happy to do so. Now, you mustn't let them know that I told you any of this—it would kill them. They are making good money on this documentary, and they've rented out the brownstone for the year. That should put them back in the black."

Tears fill my eyes. "I didn't know." I remember how hard I've been on them, and how rude, and how I'd always have some smart-aleck comment, thinking they didn't want me to be with them because I'd be in the way. But that wasn't the case at all. I think of my mom, who doesn't go to the hair salon for highlights, but does them at home—out of a box—to save money. She probably wants to look good for those business meetings when she and Dad go to pitch projects. She's not one of those moms who want to look good for the sake of looking good or to hang on to their 1980s halcyon Madonna years. She's just trying to stay in the business, stay current, stay employed.

My mother tries to give me things I want. She takes me to the Village to buy something new when she's, like, wearing the same purse she's had since the 1990s when she had a desk job at a production company.

My dad, who is a terrible handyman, fixes everything in the brownstone, and it takes him hours, and he has to keep a book propped up with the instructions, but he gets the job done—and he doesn't complain. They paint our rooms themselves, but they'd be laughing and talking as though they liked doing it—not acting a bit like they couldn't afford a painter.

I'm the most selfish, horrible person I know, and I deserve anything rotten that happens to me because I'm only worried about myself.

"Now you know." Grand opens her arms to me, and I fall into them. "You are loved, Viola Chesterton, a thousand percent."

"Thank you." I bury my face in my grandmother's neck, the safest place in the world.

"Life sucks sometimes. And sometimes the money comes and sometimes the money goes. You're rich-ish, then you're broke-ish . . . and then you hit it, and you hold on to it. And then something comes up and it's gone again. My God, these days a root canal can set you back six months." Grand sighs.

"And when you're an actress, your livelihood is subject to the whims of a director. When I go up for a part, sometimes I'm too tall or too thin, or too this or too that, or not enough or way, way too much. The goddamned theater! You can't please them! I have to live with being judged from everything from the credits on my résumé to the size of my ankles! But you—you are *not* judged, and you are *not* dismissed. You are the first thought in your mother's and father's mind in the morning and their last one before sleep."

"Did they tell you that?" I ask.

"No. But I'm a mother. And that's just the way it goes. Someday, when you're a mother, you'll know what I'm talking about. But for now, I'm asking you to open up your heart a little bit wider, and give your parents the security of knowing how happy you are here. Because I see it in you, I see how happy you are here. And your parents need to know this."

Grand is right. I am pretty happy, but I like to complain. And then of course, I like to throw on my Princess Snark tiara from time to time . . . just *because*. Those days are over. "I won't make everything about me anymore, Grand," I vow.

"Nonsense. You must. It's in the genes—you're my granddaughter, aren't you? We like a mirror. And we also like our reflection in the eyes of someone who thinks we're just yummy. But you may be too young for that yet."

"No, I have a boyfriend," I blurt.

"You do?" Grand's eyes widen.

"His name is Jared Spencer."

"Rugged name." Grand looks off in the distance and squints, as though she's seeing it up in lights. "I like it."

"He makes movies too."

"Lovely."

"You'd like him a lot."

"I'm sure I will. Now, will you do me a favor? Will you go and video doo-dad—or whatever it is—your parents and be you? Be funny and dear and sarcastic just as you are so they don't think we've ever had this conversation. Can you, on this Christmas night, make them feel good about themselves? Can you do that for your very well-preserved, young-ish Grand?"

I nod that I can. I hug Grand and I inhale the scent of her perfume. Closing my eyes tightly, I hug her hard enough for my mother to feel it halfway around the world.

"There. That's better," she says. And somehow, for real, it actually *is*.

"Mom? Dad?" I say into the camera on my computer.

"Merry Christmas!" Mom waves as Dad squeezes in. They lean forward.

"Oh my God, you totally missed it! It was the best one ever. We went to church. . . ."

"Really?" Mom's eyes widen.

"Grand cried."

"She did?" Dad is impressed.

"She didn't get her soul saved or baptized or anything, but she had a good cathartic weep. Her boyfriend is totally dreamy."

"He's a little . . . ," Mom begins.

"*Way* younger. But you should see them together. They're so natural. They read aloud from their play and made us dinner. We had so much fun. But, of course, it would have been perfect to have you here."

"Thanks." I can tell my mom is trying not to cry.

"Please don't cry. I love you so much and we'll be together next year. And this, this was, well, a very interesting Christmas. A learning experience. I want to thank you for it."

"We're just happy when you're happy."

"And I'm happy. I'm very happy." I smile.

My mother and father look at each other, and for the first time since they dumped me here, it's as if someone let the air out of them. They relax before my eyes.

My father puts his arm around my mother and together they touch the screen, and I touch it on my end.

This time I don't cry or long for them, but see myself in them. Their struggles are mine, and mine are theirs. Just the way it should be for parents and children—together as best they can be, on Christmas.

TWELVE

GEORGE AND GRAND SIT AT THE LOUNGE TABLE IN
Curley Kerner's rec room and read my script for the May
McGlynn story. George finishes first, and puts down the
script. He gets up and stretches his long legs, not giving
me any indication of whether he likes it or not.

Grand reads slowly. Finally, after what seems like a
billion years, she puts the script down and removes her
reading glasses. "George?" She looks up at him.

"I think it's very good," he says.

"So do I. But it's missing something."

"What?" I ask nervously.

"Well, you have the drama of her tragic death down
cold—you're going to film the nose of the crashed plane,
and the ghost of May McGlynn emerging from the rubble,

all of that is very visual and fine, and clearly, you know what the movie is *about*—it's about a young woman who died before she achieved her full potential . . . right?"

"Exactly." I'm so happy the script makes sense I could burst with joy.

"But we never see the world that she worked in: the world of the actress, the movie actress of her era, the film studio, the world that defines who she is—or who people thought she was."

"I can't go to Hollywood and build interior sets of silent movies."

"No, you can't. But you could do it here. A story within a story. George could play her costar and I could play her sidekick and we could improvise a scene or two from her last movie project—"

I interrupt. Suddenly I get it! "And I could film you in black-and-white and we could do a voice-over about how the movie was going to change the course of her career and how May's moment had finally arrived. She was just beginning to say something with her work, to dig deep."

"Right, right!" Grand sees what I see.

"And then . . . ," I think aloud, "it wasn't to be. Her dream died when she died. And then she was judged after her death for being young and beautiful, reduced in memory to a lush and a flapper."

"Absolutely. Had May McGlynn lived we'd be talking about her as an iconic actress of the thirties—not Bette Davis or Myrna Loy, but May McGlynn!"

"Are you in, George?" I ask.

"Sounds like fun." He shrugs.

"Okay. I'll storyboard it and then we'll film first thing in the morning."

There's nothing an artist needs more—even more than excellent tools and stamina—than a deadline.

So, I sit at my computer and, with words—*not* my chosen form of self-expression, but necessary in this instance—hammer out, moment by moment and scene by scene, what I see in my mind's eye in the telling of May McGlynn's story.

Marisol watches me from her bed, as she listens to her iPod. It doesn't even bug me when she occasionally sings a "whoo whoo" phrase aloud from Gwen Stefani. She catches herself, looks at me, mouths *I'm sorry*, and gets quiet.

I'm comforted to have a witness as I figure this thing out. This movie is now driving me with an intensity I haven't felt since September when my parents dropped me off here. Back then, all my energy went into finding my way back home, and now, everything I am, everything I know, everything I want to say is wrapped up in this movie, in getting this story just right. I am driven by the desire to make something worthwhile. And then, having made something worthwhile, I want to *win* the competition.

"Are you okay?" Marisol asks.

"Never better," I promise.

The theater in Hojo is used for assemblies, plays, and faculty meetings. It's a simple auditorium with wooden seats that fold up, and a proscenium stage with black velvet drapes that create scrims on the upstage wall of the theater. It's plain and cavernous, just what I need to fake an old Hollywood set.

I set my Canon XH A1 video camera on a tripod. Grand and George are downstairs in makeup. We looked at some old photographs of Rudolph Valentino movies, and I told them to be creative. George is wearing a tux from the costume shop, and Grand chose a lacy black evening gown, elbow-length gloves, and a short flapper wig with thick bangs and spit curls. They laughed a lot when they were trying on the old costumes.

I check my lighting. Grand and George will do voice-overs later, over the images on the Avid, so at least I don't have to worry about sound when I'm filming.

Marisol hollers from the wings. "The actors are ready."

"Places," I tell them, adjusting the lens on my camera.

George strides across the stage—he really comes alive in the lights; I can see why Grand fell for him. Then she enters. As Grand moves across the stage, she's deft, smooth, and totally willowy. Grand and George have the same reverence for the stage that Father Time had for his altar in the Loretto Chapel on Christmas Day.

Grand and George applied a pale yellow pancake makeup on their faces as a base, and then very deliberate black eyeliner and brownish lipstick. I look through the lens as I check their makeup in the light. They have the look of silent movie stars.

I come from behind the camera because not only am I the director of photography on this movie, I'm the actual director and writer, so I have to do it all. "You look amazing," I tell them. My actors sort of exhale, relieved that they've pleased me.

I put my hands in my pockets and pace in the audience by the downstage lip.

"Basically, you're going to act out the day on the set when you got the news that May McGlynn has gone down in a plane. You're to act directly into the camera and react to her death. Now, the backstory is: George, you're her lover hearing the news for the first time and,

Grand, you're May's mentor—the actress who helped her learn all about Hollywood, helped her find a place to live, all of that. Any questions?"

They shake their heads no. We've been over this a few times, and we went through the storyboard before they went in to makeup. George and Grand are quick studies.

"Now, I've only got the one camera so we'll do the more stationary stuff first, and then I'll pick it up and handhold it, which wasn't something they did back then, but in telling the story it makes it more intimate and effective."

"What do you want me to do?" Marisol asks.

"I'd like you to mark each of the bullet points on the storyboard as I film them, so we know we have what we need when we go over to the dorm to do the narration."

"No problem." Marisol takes the script and a seat by the camera.

Marisol has tears in her eyes as she watches the scene. I am moved too by the power of emotions without the aid of words. George and Grand communicate everything without talking, in that very delicate way that the great silent actors did.

I do the scene several times, covering it from various angles—Grand's point of view, then George's. Then I do something that I didn't plan. I take the camera off the tripod and head to the back of the darkened theater and I ask them to hold the position after they've heard the news about May's plane crash.

Something compels me to get this intimate scene in a wide shot. That the depth from the back of the theater just might give me scope, dramatizing the loneliness of their loss in the distance and the silence.

The single beam of light from the follow spot bleeds into the work lights. George, prostrate with grief, bends so far forward he looks like a child. Grand has her hand on his back, and it's almost as if she's guiding him toward the truth. They hold the pose for a long while.

"Cut!" I shout at long last.

George comes up from his kneeling position and Grand shakes out her legs. "You trying to kill us, Viola?" Grand bellows.

"Did we get it?" George asks.

"Oh yeah," I holler.

I'm actually energized when I get back to my room after our day of filming. I've loaded the footage into the Avid. Marisol is already asleep, beat from the rigors of filmmaking. I text Jared.

Me: Got my backstory shot today.
JS: You're amazing.

242

Me: Looks good. I had two pros though. Grand and her BF, George.

JS: You got a jump start on me.

Me: Just glad I had something to do to fill the hours.

JS: The new baby cries all night.

Me: No rest?

JS: None. But she's cute.

Me: Of course. She's your sister.

JS: LOL.

I sit back in my desk chair. Maybe it's the exhilaration I feel after a full day of filming, and maybe it's residual Christmas spirit, but I miss my BF and I want him to know it.

Me: I really miss you.

The seconds it takes for the text response to appear seems to take, like, ten years. Finally:

JS: I really miss you too. You're beautiful.

I look down at the word *beautiful* and wish for a second that it wasn't 2009, but 1809, and that the word *beautiful* was written on parchment paper with a quill pen in fancy cursive letters in indelible ink. I want this text to last forever, not scroll into cyberspace where it disappears into technowhere. I want this word to last, and even more, the feelings behind it.

JS: Are you there?
Me: Oh yeah. And I always will be.
JS: Good. Me too.

What a perfect ending to a perfect day.

Grand and George pack up his Prius and head off to Cincinnati to start rehearsals for *Arsenic and Old Lace* on Sunday as the girls return in droves to PA to start the new semester. Every girl on campus seems to be wearing a new sweater.

Before she left, Grand met Suzanne and Romy and Trish, who swears she saw Grand when she toured with the musical *On the Twentieth Century* in Chicago in 1995. Trish could find stardust in the bottom of a jar of pickles.

"I just love Grand," Marisol says wistfully. "And if I had to spend a Christmas away from my family, I'm glad it was with Grand."

"Hey . . ."

"And you."

"Thanks."

"So, Viola, I'm a little worried about your movie."

"Why?" I ask, suddenly nervous.

"I don't really understand the black-and-white footage and the voice-over. I don't get it. Why do you need it?"

"Well, Marisol. You know how a poem uses words in a spare way to describe a feeling?"

"Yeah."

"When you make a movie, you have to take the audience to a place that they can only go in a movie. So, I needed to dramatize May's 1920s life, and the best way was to show her workplace."

"But how is it all going to fit together?"

"That's the art part," I tell her.

Mrs. Carleton passes out instructions about our English lit project for second semester. She wants us to imagine a police officer comes to knock on our door after a robbery, and we are to describe to the officer how the crime transpired. It's an interesting assignment, but I have other things on my mind.

"Mrs. Carleton?" I ask her after class.

"Yes, Viola?"

"I read online that you were a theater major."

"I was. Undergrad," she replies without even looking up from her laptop.

"Did you ever do any acting?"

Mrs. Carleton straightens her spine, and it's almost as if her jeans fall into straight, pressed creases. "I was the lead in Andreyev's *He Who Gets Slapped*."

"Wow. Well, I was wondering if you'd be in my movie. I've got every role cast except the fortune-teller, and I think you'd be great."

"This is for the Midwest film project?"

"Yes, it is. I have Mrs. Zidar playing a role, my RA, Trish, is going to be Hedda Hopper in Hollywood, and my roommate Suzanne is going to be May McGlynn. We're going to film this weekend here on campus."

"Do you have a script?" she asks.

"Right here." I pull the script out of my backpack. I'm sort of thrilled she asked for the script, as this is the sign of a true actress. That of course and, once reading the script, passing on the part. But I'm not worried.

"You're Mavis the fortune-teller who begs May not to get on the plane in South Bend, but to stay until the following morning. The plane crashes, so it turns out you were right," I explain.

"This sounds like fun. Count me in."

"Great!"

"And, Viola?"

"Yes, Mrs. Carleton?"

"You still have to write the witness paper."

"Oh, I know. I wasn't bogarting for extra credit. In fact, I'm getting pretty good with the writing part because I had to write this script."

Romy has turned out to be an excellent producer. She broke down my script over three days and organized the actors. Romy made sure they had their scripts in advance, and that they knew where we were filming and how long they were needed.

Marisol pulled the most fabulous period costumes from the costume shop at Phyllis Hobson Jones Hall. Marisol found drop-waist dresses, silk stockings, cloche hats, and gloves for the actors to wear. The characters came alive as the actors put on the costumes.

The biggest surprise of all was Suzanne, who never acted in her life and who stars as May McGlynn. She was so beautiful on video, her blond hair gleaming, her long torso perfect for the costumes of the period. She made the leap from coquettish actress to tragic victim with the grace and knowing of an old pro. I can't wait for Grand to see what Suzanne did with the part.

I believe Suzanne got the bug playing May McGlynn.

The movie has definitely pulled Quad 11 together in a way that we had not counted on. It's one thing to live together in harmony, but it's something special to work together, get along, and help one another in a professional setting. I won't ever forget how the girls rallied to pitch in on this just for me.

Time has definitely flown by since everyone came back from the holidays. Class, and prepping for the movie, and then actually *filming* the movie—I can't believe it's already March! The snow has melted, leaving behind mud on the ground and a small river of slush in the gutters. Spring is trying to make its way to South Bend as purple and yellow crocuses push up through the tangled brambles of winter. The bare branches of the trees are turning the palest of green, ready to bud.

I IM Andrew. I sent him the footage from the Grand and George shoot, and I want his feedback.

Me: See my footage?

AB: Creepy, but cool.

Me: That's Grand.

AB: I know. Who's the guy?

Me: An actor.

AB: I figured.

Me: In real life, that's her boyfriend.

AB: Wow.

Me: What did you think of Suzanne playing May?

AB: Awesome.

Me: Total goddess.

AB: Total. She can act.

Me: I know.

AB: But that's also due to your gift as a director.

Me: Thanks.

AB: You really made a great short.

Me: Thanks. Why all the compliments?

AB: They're true.

Me: You rock.

AB: I know.

Me: How's Olivia?

AB: She's here right now. We teamed up on labs.

Me: Great.

I lean back and wait for Andrew to ask about Jared and me.

AB: When do you go to Toledo for the competition?

Me: Friday. Mrs. Zidar is driving me in the van. My roommates are all going too.

AB: Cool. Do you think you can win?

Me: I don't think so.

AB: How come?

Me: People are doing movies about contour farming and nuclear energy as a viable alternative source to oil. And I'm doing, like, an old-fashioned mystery.

AB: But it's really good.

Me: Thanks, Andrew.

AB: It's true.

Me: I wish you could be there.

AB: Olivia wants to know if Feldman gives a tough midterm in robotics.

Why is he talking to Olivia when he's supposed to be paying attention to me?

Me: Yes.

AB: I'll tell her.

Okay. I guess he's not going to ask me about Jared.

Me: Well, I'd better go.

AB: Check ya later.

Andrew signs off and I feel abandoned. "Huh," I say aloud.

"What's the matter?" Suzanne looks up from her desk.

"Andrew is getting weirder by the day."

"Is he still with Olivia?"

"Yep."

"Is she still running his life?"

"Now it's even worse. She's sitting right there—I don't have any confidentiality with him anymore. It's awful."

"Maybe he'll break up with her."

"I think that will never happen. It's like Andrew needed a boss. It's like he likes it."

"Whipped."

"Totally."

"Thanks for giving me a copy of the movie to send to my parents."

"Are you kidding? You totally made the movie. You were great."

"I tried," Suzanne says.

"Tried? You triumphed. You're a natural-born actress."

"Thanks to you. You told me what to do."

"Yeah, but you did it," I assure her.

Suzanne chews on the end of her pencil for a minute, then she puts it back in the cup on her desk. She looks sad. "My dad really wishes he could make the drive to Toledo."

"I know."

"It's so hard." Suzanne's eyes fill with tears.

"I get it. It's like PA is filled with girls who have most of what they need in this world, but somehow, there's something missing, and it's like we were sent here to find it."

"What am I supposed to find?" Suzanne asks.

"Well . . . I think your parents understand that you needed to be away from home so that you could focus on your studies. I think your dad, most especially, wants you to be independent."

"But why?"

"He doesn't want you to need him. He loves you, but he wants you to make it on your own. Your parents are preparing you to get along without them. And the same is true for my parents. I had to come here because they needed to work, but I also had to come here because—you were right in the beginning—I'm sheltered and I needed to learn how to stand on my own two feet."

"You're not anymore."

"I'm still pretty sheltered. But I'm not afraid anymore. I'm not afraid that I'll never go home. I'm just going to try and do my best where I am, wherever that is, and not worry about it too much."

"That's really smart."

I hear a bell ding and check my instant messages. Did

Andrew realize he was being weird and come back? No, but it's even better. "It's Jared," I announce.

Me: Can't wait to see you this weekend.

JS: Me too.

Me: I think my RA, who smiles 24/7 like Mr. Sardonicus, is coming to Toledo.

JS: I remember her. Trish.

Me: Right. I have a whole bunch of support. Do you?

JS: Yeah.

Me: Are your parents coming?

JS: Not sure.

Me: Do you want them to?

JS: Either way is okay. How did the footage of your grandmother cut with the rest?

Me: Fine. Can't wait to see your movie.

JS: Fingers crossed.

Me: Okay. Well, talk to you later.

JS: Later.

I sit back in my chair. Maybe it's me, but Andrew is acting strange and now Jared is acting just as weird. He didn't email that he was excited, or even interested to see my movie. It's like I had to pull the support out of him. Maybe he's nervous. Or maybe, like me, he wants to win

253

and he doesn't want to say that to me, since I'm also in the competition. But he told me about the contest—it's not like I found out about it on my own. Isn't that a form of support for me?

Mom always says that relationships between girls and boys are complicated, and I never believed her. Now I'm beginning to see that she's right.

Romy, Marisol, and Suzanne gather around my computer to watch the final cut of *The May McGlynn Story*. I pace behind them as the opening credits roll.

Romy will see her budget and schedule come to life on the screen, Marisol will see her costumes and set design (including the nose of the plane, which was actually an air-conditioning vent we borrowed from maintenance and jammed into the ground for wreckage) on-screen, and Suzanne, well, she's the star of the movie, and she will see herself as May McGlynn for the first time.

I was very firm about not showing them any of the movie in bits and pieces, no matter how much they begged. I wanted their pure reaction to the finished product. And now, I don't think I can take it as they watch. I stand by the windows, as far from the computer screen as I can be as they watch the movie.

The girls lean back and laugh heartily when Mrs. Zidar appears as the doctor on the scene of the crash. Mrs.

Carleton gives an understated performance as Mavis the fortune-teller who warns May it's not in her cards to have safe travel that day, while Trish gives a scenery chewing performance in her lone scene as Hedda Hopper in Hollywood as she reports on the radio that May McGlynn has died. Trish would have ended up on the cutting room floor, but unfortunately, she carried an important story point and I couldn't lose her. (Won't make *that* mistake again.)

Grand's and George's scenes are cut into the body of the action. And I even did this weird flashback thing when Mrs. Carleton looks at a deck of cards on her table: the black and white of the cards is smash cut to the black-and-white footage, and then I used this creepy music from *The Fly* (we're allowed to use it because we're not going to profit from making the movies for competition). Anyhow, it totally worked.

"Wow." Marisol looks at me as The End jumps into frame.

My roommates applaud wildly.

"You guys really like it?"

"I think it's great," Marisol says.

"I don't know how you did it," Romy marvels.

"I'm crappy," Suzanne says. "I hope I don't tank it for you."

"Are you kidding? You were amazing," I tell her.

"You're my friend. The real May McGlynn was more sparkly than me."

"No way. You're good," Romy says to Suzanne.

"I love it," Marisol says supportively. "It's compelling and original. You pack a lot into a short movie. And you did so much great work with the camera. I think you could win."

"Trish says you guys can come with me to Toledo. I hope you will."

"She'll make us sing camp songs all the way," Romy grouses. "But I can handle her."

"It's for a good cause. We have to support our sister," Marisol says.

Marisol just says that word *sister* lightly, like right off the top of her head without thinking. But all my life, I have wished for a sister. I had hoped my parents would have a baby when I was small, and then when I got to be twelve I wanted them to go to China and adopt. But Mom would always smile and say, "We have our hands full with you." And maybe she was right. But what Mom never told me is that along the way, you find sisters, and they find you. Girls are very cool that way.

I could not have made the movie without my roommates. I couldn't have stayed beyond the first week without them either. We hang out, we help one another, we tell one another our worst fears and biggest secrets, and then, just like real sisters, we listen and don't judge. And then, time and time again, in small ways and ginormous ways, they are there for me. They represent. Romy had never done a budget, Marisol had never designed costumes and sets, and Suzanne had never acted, but when I asked them to help, they didn't hesitate. They came through—like sisters. Yes, we get annoyed, and sometimes we fuss, but for the most part, we have figured out a very cool way to be family to one another. And that realization has been the best part of life at the Prefect Academy. I found Suzanne, Romy, and Marisol, and they found me.

THIRTEEN

MRS. ZIDAR PARKS THE VAN IN THE GUEST LOT AT THE University of Toledo, which is so large and rambling, with building upon building connected by swirls of sidewalks, that I'd bet the campus is as big as the city itself. Trish, who came along as a co-chaperone, wasn't annoying at all on the trip. She listened to an audiobook on the way here, and hardly said a word.

As we follow the Xeroxed flyers that say WELCOME MIDWEST SECONDARY SCHOOL FILM COMPETITION to the entrance lobby of the auditorium, I feel a little sick. It's one thing to show a movie on your computer in Curley Kerner, but it's another entirely for a bunch of strangers to watch it in a theater, blown up from a DVD. I'm sure the quality will suck, but so will everyone else's.

As the rules said, video/hi-def only. We weren't allowed to use 16mm film, which would have been pretty wondrous. Next time.

Jared and I decided not to show each other our films beforehand. Well, really, it was his choice. I would have liked his feedback, but he felt it would be inappropriate because we are in competition, and shouldn't seek each other's opinions in advance. There was nothing in the rule book that said we couldn't show our films to other contestants, but I just went with Jared's decision because he seemed so definite about it. I didn't want to *force* him to watch my movie.

We haven't had time to text or email much, as we were both working up to the final moments before the submission deadline. I have missed him, but it's a funny thing, when you have a movie due, everything else, including cute boyfriends, takes a backseat.

I stand on line in the A–Gs contemplating worst-case scenarios, like people walking out or booing my film or both, when I hear, "Hey, Viola!"

I turn. Jared stands with a group from GSA. He looks like he grew about five inches since Christmas, and he looks older in his tie and jacket. He comes right over and gives me a big hug. "How're you feeling?"

"Nervous. How about you?"

"What's gonna happen is gonna happen." He smiles. But it's not Jared's usual, sweet smile. This one is tense.

"I guess." How lame, but I don't know what to say. This is the first time I haven't known what to say to Jared Spencer, and it's off-putting to say the least.

He lowers his voice. "Sorry I've been so busy."

"That's okay. It's been nuts for me too."

"Yeah. Lot going on," he says and looks off in the distance.

"Um, there's a lecture at Saint Mary's in a couple of weeks. Susie Essman is touring with a one-woman show about comedy."

"Cool."

"The tickets are going real fast," I tell him. "I'll email you the information."

"Great. I'll see you later."

Jared goes back on the M–Z line and talks with his advisor. I have a funny feeling. He wasn't boyfriend warm; he was sort of distant. Maybe he's even more nervous than me.

"He's feeling the pressure," Marisol whispers, reading my mind. I'd been so distracted I hadn't realized my girls had come up to me.

"Don't take it personally," Suzanne says. "This is where men and women are different. We can put aside petty competition for relationships—they can't. It interferes."

"That's crazy," Romy argues. "Can't he have a girl-friend and be in a film competition at the same time?"

"No. Look. It's not as if I *like* delivering bad news about boys, but it happens to be true. Both my brothers are this way. They focus on something—like winning in track or passing an exam or saving up to buy a wreck—and it's like they have a nuclear beam on the goal until they get it done. It's just the way boys are. Jared has that look like he wants to win. In this moment, it's more important than his feelings for Viola. He's focused on a trophy."

"Well . . . ," I say quietly. "So am I." I stand up straight as I pin my plastic name tag on my sweater. "I came here to win."

We follow the line into the auditorium. I look around. In a theater that seats five hundred, it looks like there's about seventy-five of us. This is a disappointment. I imag-ined the auditorium overflowing with an audience for the premiere of *The May McGlynn Story*. I mean, this is a univer-sity—don't they care about watching student projects?

The films are fifteen minutes (tops) in length. So, we will watch the fourteen submissions in alphabetical order with one intermission in between. Then we get to vote on the Audience Award, while a panel of judges goes off to figure out who wins. At this point we get a box lunch, and then there's the awards ceremony.

Romy, Marisol, Suzanne, and I are transfixed as the movies begin. At first, the selection of entries seems amateurish, single ideas delivered without a camera move. Romy leans over and squeezes my hand. She figures we're a shoo-in.

That is until the movie *My Grandmother's Last Day*, which tells the story of a dying grandmother narrated by her granddaughter, who interviews her about her life. The filming style was simple, but the content, an African American grandmother reflecting on her life before civil rights legislation, is brilliant. The movie manages to be emotional without being sentimental. I write a note to Romy that we should vote in a block for it on the Audience Award. "We have to watch all of them first," she whispers. Romy is very fair that way.

I almost have to leave the theater when the opening credits for *The May McGlynn Story* jump onto the screen. In a second and a half, I decide that this will be the absolute last time I make a movie. I picture myself selling my camera at the Martinelli Pawn Shop on Atlantic Avenue and then, years later, working in an office at a desk job. I can't take this pressure.

The audience seems very alert throughout the

beginning, and then, when the scene with Trish jumps onto the screen, a giggle ripples through the house that turns into laughter. I didn't think my movie was a comedy. Trish is laughing too, her face in her hands, and I find that mildly insulting. I took this seriously and when I went into editing I was stuck with her crap performance, and now I see that she did the whole thing—as everything—as a happy-go-lucky lark. Lesson learned.

The laughter sort of dies down as the story cuts to the Hollywood set with George and Grand in grief. The audience barely breathes as a series of cuts lead to the wide shot of the two of them bereft on the stage. I held that shot for three seconds, a long time, and then I feel I have the audience back.

In the final scene, where May (Suzanne) walks the field as a ghost, she delivers the point of the movie: that a life lived in the movies is forever, while a life lived on earth is not. Even May McGlynn, beautiful, energetic, and talented, cannot escape the ultimate fate in life—death waits for all of us. May says, "I was just a girl like you, from Indiana, who got a little lucky and then one day that good luck turned. Live in the moment, because that's all you have for certain."

There's a burst of applause when my movie ends. I use the last seconds of the darkened theater as the credits roll to run to the girls' room. I get inside and throw water on my face. How do my parents do this? I wonder. *Why* do they do it? And why do they keep doing it over and over again? This is horrible.

Romy pushes through the door, followed by Suzanne and Marisol. "Are you okay?" Marisol asks.

"I should never have entered it in the competition. And to be up there after that perfect grandmother movie. I'm lucky they didn't throw tomatoes." I begin to cry.

Marisol yanks hard, brown paper towel squares out of the silver dispenser. "Here."

The brown paper cannot soak up my tears. It's like weeping into a brick. Suzanne, Marisol, and Romy gather around me as I sob. Soon, I'm embarrassed that I'm crying—after all, the girl in the grandmother movie lost her *grandmother*. I just embarrassed myself with a lousy short-subject movie. I don't have a *real* problem. Not really.

The girls don't say much as I wash my face. The door pushes open and two professors around my mom's age enter and go into the stalls.

"The grandmother piece was a wonderment," one of the ladies says.

"God yes," the other one says.

I turn to go and Romy stops me, putting her finger to her lips.

"And what did you think of May McGlynn?" one of the ladies asks.

"It was ambitious."

"But it was really about something," the other one says.

"The black-and-white footage was amazing."

"It's a contender for sure."

Suzanne quietly opens the door and we sneak back out into the hallway. "See, they liked it. Whoever they are!"

"I know how hard this is," Romy says. "But you have to believe in yourself, stand up for your hard work. You did a great job."

Out in the lobby the students gather at the dough-nuts and cider table talking about the movies. I see Jared across the crowd, talking with a couple of film students from the university. He does not look my way.

"You guys want doughnuts?" Suzanne asks.

"Let's go wait in the auditorium." I'm not feeling like socializing. The last person I want to see is Jared, and yet, there was a part of me that hoped he would be wait-ing outside the girls' bathroom. I even looked for him.

We go back into the auditorium and take our seats, not saying much. Jared's film is up after the intermission.

Romy listens to her iPod while Suzanne checks her BlackBerry. Marisol fishes in her tote and rips into a jumbo-sized Kit Kat, snapping off a piece for each of us.

Soon, people start to filter back in. The audience seems way smaller than it did before the intermission. I'm glad my movie was shown in the first half—at least I had the max that the U of T had to offer in terms of audience bodies.

Jared comes down the far aisle, looking around. I wave to him. He gives me a thumbs-up, and I mouth *Good luck* to him. He goes back to his seat down front, joining his group from GSA.

Jared's opening credits roll. I can see he used the Avid update that I gave him. His titles are crisp and well placed. Then his story of organic farming unfolds. The shots are steady, but the movie comes across as one of those dry news b-rolls. There's an interesting farmer in the movie, but there's not enough of him. Romy squeezes my hand. Suzanne leans over. "This is boring," she whispers.

As the movie ends, at the fifteen-minute mark to the second, it feels as though three hours have passed. Serviceable and full of content, his film lacked a story, and the flat political point of view didn't show a dramatic arc. There was no tension. Jared Spencer is not a compelling storyteller. And furthermore, he didn't ask me to sit with him, and he didn't make it his business to come over and tell me my movie was good (even if he thought it sucked), so I'm wondering now if the whole story of him and me is just a mirage. Before the theater went dark, he was my boyfriend. But now?

We sit through the final films, the best of which is the story of a woman who built a bomb with things she found at a beauty salon, and my favorite, a funny short about a singing cat.

The lights come up as they pass out the box lunches. I look down at Jared, who has gone over to speak with the judges. As seriously as I take this competition, Jared has taken it to a different level. He's down there schmoozing for his film. I don't think that's fair.

The box lunch was a blur. I couldn't eat for nerves. I don't want my name to be called and yet I'll die if they don't call my name. I think there was a lot of good stuff in my movie. I didn't try to be slick—I just tried to be creative. I attempted to be true to May McGlynn, to tell her story.

If my mother and father were here, they'd reassure me that it's all about making art and letting it live—not snuffing the essence out with ego. But I have an ego! And I want more than anything to win a prize for my work!

When the college girl with the basket comes by to collect our votes for the Audience Award, we vote in a block for the grandmother movie. I hope that girl wins first place, not that it will make up for her grandmother being dead, but it would at least cheer her up a little.

I look down at Jared, who is hunkered down in his seat with his fist clenched against his lips. I can't believe this is the same boy who was so sweet to me, who found a ride in a blizzard to give me a Christmas present, and who told me about this very competition without an ounce of envy. The Jared Spencer I see now is self-involved and just a little mean. I needed his support today, and it was the last thing he was ready or willing to give.

Mrs. Zidar and Trish slip into two open seats behind us, each of them giving me a squeeze on my shoulders. Mrs. Zidar, who I found annoying in her mom jeans at the freshman picnic, has actually become a mentor I can count on. And Trish, even though she's a terrible actress and way too upbeat, at least tries. And, I must say, they are there for me. What more could I ask for?

The judges begin to read the awards. Marisol, Romy, Suzanne, and I are holding hands. The technical award goes to the singing cat, and then they award the top four movies, beginning with the honorable mention. The girl who filmed a woman making bombs in the beauty salon wins it. She goes up to the stage and stands. Then, the judge, who looks like an exhausted teacher on the verge of retirement, reads third place: It goes to a guy who made a film about three generations of Miss Corn pageant winners from the Midwest County Fair. It was really funny.

"No way we're getting anything," I promise them.

"Second place—Viola Chesterton for *The May McGlynn Story*."

Romy, Marisol, and Suzanne jump up and start screaming. I just sort of freeze and think I might faint. I feel the wedge of Kit Kat chocolate at the top of my throat. I can't breathe.

"Go, go!" Trish pushes me.

"Go up there!" Mrs. Zidar says.

I walk down the aisle. My legs feel like overcooked spaghetti and I wish I had put on some lip gloss in the bathroom. I go to the side of the stage and walk up the stairs. Each step feels like I have concrete in my Verve wedge boots. The judge looks at me, like "Hurry up, kid, I have a class to get to" so I sort of skip to him and accept my trophy. I look down into the audience and the first person I see is Jared, who is kind of smiling, but applauding very slowly, like just three big claps, not a lot of small ones to make noise. I look back at my roommates, who are still screaming and jumping for joy.

"Settle down there, girls," the judge says into the

microphone. "And now, the first-place winner in the Midwest Secondary School Film Competition is Chevon Brickey for *My Grandmother's Last Day*."

Cheers erupt from the middle of the auditorium as Chevon makes her way to the stage. She deserved to win, and I'm happy to be second place to her movie. She comes up the stairs. The other winners gather around her.

"And now the Audience Award." The judge takes the envelope from the professor seated in the first row of the auditorium. "Chevon Brickey for *My Grandmother's Last Day*."

The audience applauds loud and long for the winner. Chevon holds up her trophies as her mom and teachers come down to the edge of the stage to take her picture. Mrs. Zidar and Trish and Marisol and Romy and Suzanne get out their cell phones and click away as I stand with the winners.

I look at the trophy. It's an old-fashioned movie clapper with brass stripes. Evidently they will engrave our names on them later. I think of the clapper that Jared gave me for Christmas and how, because he had given it to me, I thought about him when I filmed a scene. I want to thank him for that.

I look down into the audience where Jared is sitting, and his seat is empty. He is gone.

FOURTEEN

THE CONSORTIUM OF SCHOOLS WANTS US TO POSE FOR pictures for the online magazine, so I stand with the winners and have my picture taken about a billion times. I am so thrilled, but my happiness is definitely brought down a notch by thoughts of Jared.

To be fair, I didn't spring out of my chair and go down to *him* after they showed his movie. It was very polished, and I could have said *that*, but I don't want to be a phony. He made a very dry movie, and it made me not want to visit an organic farm. Ever. But he is my sort-of boyfriend, and I should put aside my judgments and support him.

I give Marisol the trophy to hold and go up the aisle and out into the lobby. They've put out punch and the remaining doughnuts from the morning break, along with pecan sandy cookies from the package on plastic platters. I look around through the crowd and I see Jared from behind standing by the windows. I thread through the crowd to get to him.

When I squeeze my way through, I am stunned. Jared is standing with his arm around a very pretty girl who appeared in the beauty parlor bomb movie as a customer. She has waist-length red hair with a forest-green velvet ribbon threaded through it. She whispers in his ear and he laughs.

My face burns hot with embarrassment. They must've felt my stare because they turn. The place is so packed that I can't get out of there and besides, it's too late. Jared Spencer, of two dates, one lecture, five kisses, one cookie, one book, and one movie clapper says, "Viola."

"I was just checking to see how you were."

"Congratulations." His congratulations feel empty.

"I'm Viola Chesterton." I extend my hand to the pretty girl.

"I'm Zane Pierpont," she says.

"You were great in the beauty parlor bomb movie."

"Thanks." She smiles.

"I could've used you in my movie. My RA really sucked as Hedda Hopper."

There's an awkward silence that I am inclined to fill

with a lie. "You did a great job on your movie, Jared. I thought it was very compelling."

"Thanks," he says. "This competition wasn't about serious subjects, so I got slammed. But that's okay, I'll be back next year."

I turn to go; clearly he doesn't want to talk to me. But then, his words settle in—he actually thinks he deserved to win? Jared Spencer cannot see himself in any context other than first place. He isn't happy for the winners, so he feels compelled to diss the entire competition. That's not fair. I turn back.

"I thought there were a lot of serious movies. The first-place winner, for example."

"Total sentimental favorite," he says dismissively.

"I thought the emotions in it were very real."

Zane Pierpont shifts uncomfortably, like she doesn't want to talk about movies, unless she's in them; otherwise she's bored.

"It played to the crowd," Jared says.

"Well, I trust the audience," I fire back.

"Good for you," he says, looking into the eyes of Zane Pierpont, his new girlfriend of, like, five and a half seconds. He rolls his eyes and she laughs. Now, if this were Brooklyn, and I was at LaGuardia, I'd just hold up my hand and say "Whatever," but we're in Toledo and

I worked really hard on my movie and while it wasn't perfect, it was mine. And my mom and dad taught me to stand up for what I believe in, so Jared is about to get a little honesty, New York style.

"Maybe you should listen to the audience. They were asleep during your movie. It was the most boring one in the competition. But that's because you think you know more than anyone else about the technical side of film-making. But I have a newsflash for you, Jared Spencer, you don't know anything about feelings. And feelings are what make art."

I don't wait for his response, because in this moment I just broke up with my first boyfriend—in public—and my face burns hot like it's a boiling egg. I turn and see that Romy, Suzanne, and Marisol have heard the whole thing and created a wall of support behind me.

"Let's go," Marisol says, handing me the trophy.

We turn and push through the crowd and walk outside into the fresh air. Mrs. Zidar and Trish are already waiting in the van.

"Are you okay?" Suzanne asks.

I should feel awful. After all, I really liked him, but that's before I *knew* him.

"I'm fabulous!" I tell my roommates. "Never better!"

Romy, Suzanne, and Marisol high-five and laugh.

"You won second place!" Romy says.

"It feels really good," I say as we pile into the van.

"Okay, girls, we thought Red Lobster for the victory dinner," Mrs. Zidar says.

"Bring it on," I tell her.

When we drive onto the campus of the Prefect Academy, it's after midnight. I called Grand and George (they opened to rave reviews in Cincinnati; Grand says the revival will run forever and there will be a national tour), who were thrilled. I called Mom and Dad, who were totally happy and wanted every detail, including my take on every other movie in the competition.

The girls and I spent a lot of time on the ride home talking about Jared Spencer. They marvel at how well I'm handling it, but the truth is, when I look back, especially while we were making our movies, Jared was distant. The emails became shorter and shorter, and the texts fewer and fewer. I chalked it up to being busy and in production, but maybe he was already planning on breaking up with me. He didn't want me to be the best I could be, and I only want to be the best I can be. It just took me winning second place and him going home empty-handed to finalize the break.

I wanted to get to six kisses. I really did. I felt that

275

five was a murky number, hovering between sort-of boy-friend and real boyfriend. Six would sort of seal the deal, I had thought in my mind. But all in all, it was a good first relationship, and I learned a lot.

Marisol can't understand why I'm not more upset. I probably would be, if I hadn't won second place. A prize for a film I made has definitely taken the edge off my grief in losing my very first boyfriend. I also know that boys are boys. They can never be true sisters. Ever. I believe in Suzanne's philosophy—you can't get too crazy about this, because boys *are* different, and you can't trust them with your feelings. Maybe not *all* boys. I mean, I trust Andrew, for example.

Mrs. Zidar drops us off in front of Curley Kerner, where Mr. Simpson, head of security, lets us in to go up to our quad. Trish follows us up the stairs. We tiptoe down the hallway, not wanting to wake anyone. When we get to our room, we hear "Surprise!" All the girls on our floor are in our quad with a big sign that says CON-GRATULATIONS, VIOLA!

I don't know what to say. I'm so overwhelmed. I pass the trophy around and the girls scream and marvel at it, so proud that their classmate went to Toledo and actually won something.

* * *

I IM Andrew even though it's late.

Me: I won second place!

AB: Oh man, that is fantastic! Good for you!

Me: It was really fun.

AB: Your movie is great and you deserved to win! I didn't know if those chuckleheads in the Midwest would know quality when they saw it. But they did! Brooklyn rules in South Bend, Indiana.

Me: Imagine that!

AB: You did—and you won! Whoo-hoo.

Me: Thanks. Now do you want the bad news?

AB: You okay?

Me: Kind of.

AB: What's wrong—stop typing and call me.

Me: No, keep typing.

AB: Okay.

Me: I broke up with Jared Spencer. He freaked when I won and he didn't and I went out to talk to him after the competition and he hooked up with this pretty redhead named Zane Pierpont (like, what kind of a name is that?). Anyhow, it was kind of humiliating, but I told him that his movie sucked because he dissed all the winners and I don't know if he got mad or whatever because we just left right away.

AB: Good for you for taking a stand.

Me: I thought so.

AB: I'm sure his movie sucked.

Me: Well, I thought so.

AB: I have news too.

Me: What?

AB: I broke up with Olivia.

I stop typing for a minute. Huh.

Me: Why?

AB: She was, like, running my life. She made me do stuff—like make plans every weekend—and, like, take her to the library and then right after, to the nail salon. I would almost choke to death in that nail salon from the fumes. Breathing in there can't be good for people. And then she'd want to run errands. She has, like, more errands than a boatload of girls. She runs errands all day on Saturday and it, like, eats up the entire day.

Me: I'm sorry.

AB: It's not fun hanging out with her, like it is with you.

I sit back in my chair. As much as I liked Jared, he was never as much fun as Andrew. Jared never read my mind. And shouldn't a boyfriend be able to?

Me: Thanks. I'll be home for the summer.

AB: *Can't wait.*

Me: BFFAA.

AB: *Oh yeah. Vi?*

Me: Yeah.

AB: *One more thing. IM Caitlin.*

Me: She's not allowed.

AB: *Her mom said she could tonight—because of the contest. So go ahead and IM her. She's waiting.*

I click over to Caitlin's email and IM her.

Me: Caitlin, it's me, how did you score getting your mom to let you IM?

CP: *I have to do laundry for a month. Just kidding! Mom knows I couldn't wait to talk to you about the movie. What happened?*

Me: I won second place!

CP: *OMG!*

Me: I know!

CP: *And you're coming home soon. Andrew misses you—and so do I!*

Me: And I miss you guys.

CP: *What are you going to do about Jared? Wait for college?*

Me: It's O-VUH.

CP: *Why?*

279

Me: He dropped me—got all jealous of my movie.

CP: His loss!

Me: You think?

CP: Totally. Okay, Mom breathing in the doorway.

Me: Go!

CP: Got it.

Me: LOL.

CP: LOL.

My parents are driving out to pick me up today, and I realize, with the spring fling, the charity auction, and midterms, and then finals, I haven't kept up at all with my video diary. Now, maybe my mom will give me a pass because I made an actual movie—but a deal's a deal and I always honor my commitments.

I take out my camera in the field in front of the Prefect Academy, and fill the frame with the lush greenery of Indiana in late spring. You can smell the grass and first buds of corn that have the scent of sweet earth. The sun is shining way high in the sky, looking like a gold button on a sea of blue. There's not a cloud to be seen.

I film the sign:

THE PREFECT ACADEMY FOR YOUNG WOMEN
SINCE 1890

Then the microphone picks up my voice in narration.

"I have enjoyed my ninth-grade year at the Prefect Academy. Next week, I turn fifteen and this fall, I'll be back at LaGuardia and hanging out with Andrew, and life will be normal again. I'm going to miss Romy and Suzanne and especially Marisol, who understands me in a way that I thought only Andrew could. It's been very cool here."

I film the buildings and the glass atriums between them. Outside Curley Kerner, cars are jammed with parents picking up their daughters, filling trunks with boxes and suitcases and the odd sculpture or painting or science project.

I walk to the creek by the bend and instead of being all gnarly and gross as it was in September, crystal water rushes over the rocks like ribbons of pale-blue satin. I film the rushing water for a long time.

Then I turn to get one last shot of the field. I do a slow pan and try to catch the depth of the field and the first shoots of the stalks of corn rising beyond it to the farm in the next acreage. The color gold has never been so brilliant, or as shimmering as the 24K necklaces that the Brooklyn girls wear with such style.

And then, on the far edge of the field, something red moves in the gold. It's almost as if the landscape is splashed with a quick shot of red ink. I keep the camera on and hold it steady, but look from behind the lens with both eyes and squint. The red goes—it must have been a bird, I think. That, or May McGlynn is officially moving on—just like me.

I walk back to the dorm to wait for my parents, due to arrive any moment. I look down at my feet. This morning I went deep into my closet and pulled out my bright yellow patent leather Verve flats to wear on the trip east. I haven't worn them much in Indiana; they're way too bright and say New York like nothing else can . . . or did. But they're just right for today, just right for going home.

ACKNOWLEDGMENTS

My evermore thanks to the great team at HarperTeen. I am lucky to work with a fabulous editor, Tara Weikum. Laura Kaplan is a publicity whiz. Thank you also to the brilliant Susan Katz, Kate Jackson, Elise Howard, Jocelyn Davies, Barb Fitzsimmons, Alison Donalty, Ray Shappell, Diane Naughton, Cristina Gilbert, Erin Gallagher, Kristina Radke, Colleen O'Connell, Laura Kaplan, Marisa Wetzel, Andrea Pappenheimer, Kerry Moynagh, Kathy Faber, Liz Frew, Jessica Abel, Josh Weiss, Melinda Weigel, and Barbara Cho.

At the powerhouse William Morris Endeavor Entertainment my daily gratitude to: Suzanne Gluck, Nancy Josephson, Cara Stein, Michelle Bohan, Alicia Gordon, Jennifer Rudolph Walsh, Sarah Ceglarski, Liz Tingue, Caroline Donofrio, Natalie Hayden, Philip Grenz, Erin Malone, Eliza Chamblin, Tracy Fisher, Eugenie Furniss, Cathryn Summerhayes, Raffaella de Angelis, and Josh Levy.

Thank you to Larry Sanitsky, the great producer who reads often and early, and at the Sanitsky Company: Jay Steckel and Claude Chung.

I am most lucky to have the world's best assistant, Kelly Meehan. And thank you also to Molly McGuire who swoops in and works hard when we need her the most.